SOLDIER OF PRIDE

TOSSIA MITCHELL

This is a work of fiction. Names, characters, places, and incidents are products of the author's imagination or are used fictitiously and are not to be construed as real. Any resemblance to actual events, locations, organizations, or persons, living or dead, is entirely coincidental.

Table of Contents

DULCE ET DECORUM ESTE

We are brothers.
We have fought side by side,
Walked the same road,
Felt the same enemy.
We know each other in the darkest of night
And the deepest of sorrows.
We have shared the sullenness of hell.
Together, we have experienced
The impieties of war.
For I am called "Soldier,"
And he…
He is called "Fear."
Tossia Mitchell

DEDICATION

This book is dedicated to my father, who bravely fought for freedom, and to my brother, with love and memories. Without you, I could never have dreamed.

INTRODUCTION

For you to fully understand my story, I need to start at the beginning. I am a person who has always craved people and learning. It's like a fire raging through my veins that never subsides. I am constantly craving fuel to stoke it—searching, needing more, and always questioning.

During a conversation I recently had with a friend, I was described as a "contributor." It was then that it became clear to me that I am a vast sea; I need rivers to flow and feed into me, so I can exist. Thus, I crave people and knowledge; I have an uncontrollable desire to constantly discover and learn. I don't long to learn in a traditional manner, such as receiving a diploma or doctorate. I want to learn about life, people, and their hearts.

With the awareness of this definition of my character came the realization that I'm selfish. In fact, I use people to fuel my needs. It bothered me to think that I could be a person who uses others for my own satisfaction.

After deep contemplation, I became aware that while I take from people, I also give back. I give something of myself to each person that I encounter. Can this exchange be so wrong? I give others small glimmers of hope and understanding, moments of happiness, and insight into their hearts, dreams, and desires. No promises, no commitments. Just a feeling of self-worth and a sharing of dreams.

In doing so, I steal a small part of one's heart to be held in my hands. Then once again, destiny brings us to a fork in the road, where we will go our separate ways. Some pass by quickly — like shadows in the dark — while others pull up a chair and stay a little while. How long one decides to stay in my presence depends entirely on the needs of that particular individual. Therefore, what I give and receive is completely up to them.

CHAPTER 1
THE OLD WOMAN, KOSOVO

She said, "What can a bird do to stop the wind?"

The young soldier stood numb as he felt the words strike his heart like a hot knife, piercing and twisting as it dug deeper and deeper into the center of the steel harshness of his existence.

Yet he had experienced war. He had witnessed the horror and scandalous injustice it brings. He had seen bloodshed. He had walked through the streets of Kosovo, which were scattered with purple-gray rotting bodies. He had seen their dismantled limbs being picked up and shoved into black garbage bags.

He had lost count of how many children he had pulled off their dead mothers and fathers. After their tiny fingers finally let go, they could only hold tightly to him as they succumbed to the fear that rampaged through them.

This strong soldier had comforted sobbing grandmothers as he tore them away from the remains of their bombed homes. He had soothed their broken hearts as he guided them to the trucks to be herded away to the compounds like oblivious cattle.

He had pushed the dismantled guts of young soldiers back into their bodies as he held them tightly, making promises only

9

God could keep.

And yet the words of the old woman had shaken him. But perhaps it was not the actual words, but what they represented.

The question lingered before him. He was somehow both credulous and dubious.

"What can a bird do to stop the wind?"

It was a simple question, yet it saturated the air with a deep, desolate helplessness. The soldier waded through the emotions that suddenly stood tall and impregnable, like the stone walls of the Bastille.

He stared at the old, jaded woman, whose past was trapped in a corner of her memory, faded and torn. He was frozen to the spot, paralyzed, like the statues of the Acropolis. The agony he felt from the old woman tore at him with the sharp talons of a hawk, ripping the very flesh from his soul.

History was clearly visible on the woman's haggard face. The serration of her skin was deeply etched with the story of her fate; the dark crevasses of her life were evident for all to see.

For the old woman and the young soldier, time remained motionless. Her eyes were numb and void. The empty gaze of this drowned woman made him uneasy. She didn't blink or move.

The soldier began to squirm uneasily like a specimen under a microscope. His breathing grew faster. He didn't realize the impact this moment would have on his being. It would remain unremittingly branded into his memory, and become a scar so deep that its effects would last the duration of his lifetime. A scar, not visible to the eye, but planted deeply in his memory, branding his soul until only death could release it.

Chapter 2
THE ENCOUNTER

It was a very slow night on my computer. At that point, I hadn't encountered anyone interesting. I was about to log off when I received a personal message from a young man. As we started talking, I discovered he was an American soldier stationed in Kosovo.

At first, he was extremely arrogant and angry. I usually try to avoid this type of person on the Internet, but something drew me to him. It wasn't anything in particular—just a feeling that someone has about someone else, a drawing of souls. He was young yet old, sensitive yet cold, educated yet crass.

Yes, this young man definitely intrigued me. He'd grabbed my attention. I needed to know: What'd triggered the anger? What created the huge stonewall that he hid behind?

During our lifetimes, many people cross our paths, and I've often wondered why certain individuals have crossed mine. On this particular night, I questioned the reason why I'd met this soldier.

11

Chapter 3
THE CONFLICT

You all think you're so great, sitting in your warm, comfortable homes.

The words appeared hostile and rude as they sat on my computer screen.

Are you talking to me?

I was shocked at the words that jumped out at me. I'd been busy conferring with my friends online, sharing the day's tribulations with each other. Then the message appeared. I was annoyed.

Who are you? Why are you bothering me?

No answer came. I waited. Still no reply.

What did I do to you to make you so angry at me?

Hard and fast, the stranger responded.

All you people out there think everything is just fine, while we're over here fighting and killing and dying.

12

I gazed at the words. I wondered why he'd chosen me, a complete stranger. What could've happened that'd make him feel like he had to lash out at someone like this?

He angrily continued, swearing and blaming.

My face turned red from the obscenities. How dare he bother me? How dare he talk to me like that?

Does your mother know what you're saying on here? She'd be ashamed of you, talking to strangers like that. If you want to behave in that way, I suggest you go find someone else to yell at.

I felt better after telling him off. Now maybe he'd leave me alone. I'd heard about incidents happening online, but I'd never personally encountered one before. I was caught off-guard. And now I was hopping mad that someone would get online and speak to me so ignorantly.

What's your problem, lady?

I imagined this arrogant stranger, laughing at his computer, thinking he was funny. It made me furious.

You're my problem, young man! How old are you anyway?

Thoughts raced through my mind. This "young man" must really be a group teenagers playing an online prank while their parents were out.

I'm thirty years old, and I'm a soldier in Kosovo.

Sure you are. And I'm the Prime Minister of Canada. Please leave me alone.

At last my computer was quiet. I was glad he was gone. The evening's mood was ruined, so I decided to say goodnight to my friends.

As I reached to turn off my computer, his words appeared again.

You don't even know what's happening on this side of the world. Just go ahead and laugh. They all do.

You're rude for a man of thirty. You should be ashamed of yourself. If you're a soldier as you say, then you're a disgusting representation of your country!

I regained my composure.

If you want to be rude, I'm going to block you. Then I won't have to receive these insulting propositions from you.

I felt better after I'd warned him.

I liked being online, meeting people, making friends from all over the world, and learning about the areas they live in.

Are you there?

He was back. I ignored him. This man was rude and persistent. I didn't want anything to do with him. Or did I?

Are you there? he repeated.

Yes, but I don't want to talk to the likes of you. You have bad manners, and you're bothering innocent people.

I shook my head and reached for my cup of tea. Why was I even bothering to answer him? I was fed up. I reached over to hit the block button, but he stopped me.

Look, I'm sorry.

Something kept me from shutting off my computer. What was it that drew me to him?

14

I didn't mean to be rude to you.

I was still sulking, so I decided not to reply. His words stirred the curiosity in me. Yet at the same time, I knew I had to be very cautious with who I spoke to online. Not everyone is real, so it can be dangerous.

Are you still there?

I'm debating whether I want to accept your apology or block you.

This time, *he* didn't reply.

I think I'm going to sign off, I snapped.

Don't go. Please don't go. I'm sorry. I had no right to get online and be rude to you. You're right. It was uncalled for. I really am sorry.

His words had the sound of someone who was reaching out. I hesitated. Almost pleading, he continued.

I've had a really bad day, and I need to talk to someone.

He sounded sincere, but I still wasn't sure. After all, you can be anyone you want to be online. My emotions were torn between curiosity and anger.

I really am a soldier in Kosovo, and I've had a rough day. I just needed to vent.

Well, you certainly don't know how to vent appropriately—especially to a stranger. I should report you.

I don't know why I did that. I really am sorry. Can we just talk for a bit? I promise I won't be rude anymore.

I didn't answer him. Now I wanted him to squirm.

I really need to talk to someone tonight. Please, I don't want to be alone. I mean, if that's all right.

His plea was enough to crumble my defenses. What could it hurt to talk a little? And if he was real, then perhaps it would help him. And if he wasn't who he said he was, I would soon find out and block him. Besides, I had a feeling in my gut that he was telling the truth. Perhaps he really did need someone to talk to. It's strange how you can actually "feel" someone's emotions online.

"Okay. But if you become rude or snap at me, I will definitely block you, and I'll report you. Don't misunderstand me: I will report you.

There, that was definitive. I sat back and waited.

I promise I won't. Thank you. I appreciate you taking the time to talk to me.

Quite the turnaround in attitude. I was pleased at the way I'd handled the situation.

What would you like to talk about?

One of my men committed suicide tonight.

Speechless, I just stared at the screen. I never could've imagined that he'd reply like that.

I'm sorry. I don't know what to say.

I shouldn't be bothering you with this. After all, you're a stranger, and you don't need all this crap.

No, no, it's okay. I don't mind. I'm a great listener.

After a long pause, he simply typed, *Thanks.* Then there was another long silence.

Are you still there?

Now it was my turn to wonder if he'd talk to me. Ironic, I thought to myself.

Yes.

Do you want to talk about it?

Not sure.

Okay.

My fingers sat on the keys. I was trying to think of what to say next. What would ease the pain that I could unmistakably feel in his words? I'd never been in this situation before.

Maybe this was a mistake.

The suicide?

No.

I waited for him to continue.

Talking to me about this?

Now I didn't want to lose him. I wanted to be there for him. He obviously needed someone. Suddenly, I knew what to say.

What could it hurt to talk? You don't know me. I don't know you. And we don't even know each other's real names. Now I was rambling. *We don't know anything about each other, so it's safe. They're just words on the computer. It's totally safe to tell me how you feel, especially on here.*

A few minutes passed, and I wondered if he was still online.

Yeah, you're right about that.

17

I could imagine him smiling now. I could see him sitting in his bunker.

So you can tell me anything you want, and you don't have to worry about me repeating it to anyone.

Okay. Thanks.

You're welcome.

I sipped my tea, waiting. It was strange, but I could visualize him. He was a handsome, strong soldier, but his shoulders were far too small to carry out the orders of the day. He was a young man who had too many responsibilities for his age. I saw a person who was sensitive, yet wasn't allowed to feel. Yes, it was strange how a few words on a computer could paint a vivid picture.

The kid was only nineteen years old. Too young to end his life.

Nineteen years old. My heart skipped a beat. My youngest daughter was older than that. I wondered how it happened and why. I didn't realize how young the soldiers in Kosovo were. My father had served in WWII. He'd told me many stories about young boys who'd died. I'd never thought about the ages of soldiers during peacetime. The number kept repeating in my head: nineteen.

Too young, he repeated.

I swallowed hard to release the lump that'd formed in my throat.

There was blood everywhere!

He was reliving the event. I sat in the darkened hush of the room. My mind was scrambling for words. An eerie silence hung in the air.

It should never have happened. I have to inform his parents.

I could feel the military precision emerging.

That's hard.

I knew the words I'd just typed were inadequate. I thought about how I'd feel if I received the news that my son was dead. How would I handle telling a parent that their nineteen-year-old son was never coming home again? They'd never be able to hold him in their arms and tell him how much they loved him. I thought of all the things I'd never said to my children—things I should've said.

Then I thought about how this young man's parents would feel when they realized their son's death was a suicide. Not shot in the line of duty. Not a hero. No medal for bravery. A shameful suicide. I felt sick.

I had to clean the mess up. But he did it in the shower, so at least I could rinse all the blood away.

I couldn't even begin to understand what my soldier was feeling at that moment. I was shocked. I could feel his grief—blaming himself for the suicide. That wasn't right. I wanted to console him.

It wasn't your fault.

My mind raced as I visualized the gruesome scene. An incident. Yes, it was just that, an incident. Plain and simple. It was something you could put in a shoebox and shove in the closet. I mulled over the word "incident."

How do you know?

My soldier's words were angry as they pounded out onto the

screen.

You weren't there.

I was taken aback by his sudden abruptness. Anger erupted in me. Not anger toward my soldier, but anger about the fact that we were sending teenagers to war.

I know I wasn't there, and neither were you! You didn't know he was going to do this, so how could you stop him?

Yeah? I should know my men. They depend on me to protect them.

So you should know what everyone is thinking, and be able to prevent everything bad that happens? Wow, you must be an amazing secret weapon for the military.

I was being sarcastic, in hopes that he would realize it wasn't his fault. He didn't kill the young boy. He had no control over what'd happened. Why was he blaming himself?

There was no reply. I sat waiting. Perhaps I shouldn't have said that to him. I was criticizing him—telling him who was right and who was wrong. I breathed a sigh of relief when I saw the next words appear on my screen.

I'm laughing.

He understood my sense of humor. At that moment, I knew that we understood each other, and that was good.

When I chose you, I really got myself a feisty one, didn't I?

It made me feel better that I could lighten his mood. I visualized him laughing.

You bet you did. Maybe you should've thought twice before you were rude to me. Now it's payback time.

I laughed out loud, then continued.

You sound like a wonderful soldier. You're caring and concerned about your men. Don't blame yourself. If you do, it'll eat at you until you're not a good mentor for the rest of your men anymore. They need you.

It was obvious that he was contemplating my words.

You're right, but I just can't help thinking that I could've prevented it.

I know it's natural to think that — to blame yourself. You couldn't prevent it, and you can't undo what's been done. All you can do is try to make tomorrow better than today.

Thanks.

You're welcome.

His reply was as short as mine.

I stared at the computer screen. Exhaustion filled me. It was if we'd been in a huge battle, and I'd finally won. We were together, side by side. And at that moment, I knew we had a bond. Our friendship was going to be deep and personal.

Gotta go. It's late here. Or early, almost morning.

Find me if you need to talk again. I've got really big shoulders.

I feel better now.

I smiled.

Hey you....

Yes?

I'm glad I found you.

I'm glad you did too.

Night.

I signed off, leaned back in my chair, and stared at the blank screen. Although the conversation had been short, I was emotionally exhausted. It'd been a strange evening. Yet somehow, I knew that our paths were meant to cross.

I hoped that my soldier would find me again. If he did, I hoped I could help him — even if just for a short time. As I shut off the kitchen light, I knew tomorrow would be a better day.

Chapter 4
The Lion Tamer

After a few exchanges, my young soldier started softening toward me like a lion hypnotized by his trainer. Slowly and cautiously, he opened up his heart and told me more about his short stay in Kosovo. I was careful not to overstep any boundaries of privacy; from experience, I knew that would chase him off. I realized that he would have to be treated like a scared, wounded animal—slowly gaining his trust one step at a time, never infringing on his territory, allowing him to come to me.

I sat reading as he gradually revealed his life as a soldier in Kosovo. A little at a time he relayed his story. I wanted nothing more than to reach out and take him in my arms, and tell him everything was going to be all right. I'd never expected to encounter such a tale, and it left me with a feeling of helplessness. I had no words to offer him.

His pain and heartache were so real. His harshness was embedded so deeply within him that even time wouldn't mend the hurt he was feeling.

I sat across from him. Only a computer separated us. I was aching to reach through the screen and try to heal him. But most of all, I wanted to give him a feeling of peace. For the moment, I wanted to be a mother figure who'd tuck him safely in his bed. I needed to reach out, gently stroke his head, and relay dreams of beauty and happiness that would momentarily mask the agony within his soul. Give him words that'd ease the agony and pain that tormented him. But most of all, I wanted to banish the ghost that stood in the wings, waiting for his cue.

I sat alone in the darkness of my kitchen. For the first time in my life, I had no words to offer.

CHAPTER 5
THE TRENCH

His voice could be heard loud and clear in the wet morning fog. Walking up the line, he could see his men shoveling the unbeatable wet mud; it slid back into the hole as quickly as they dug it out.

"Okay men, dig yourself in!" he commanded.

Sarge knew that danger was lurking. The rain was a definite deterrent, and now the fog was rolling in, obscuring their view of the enemy line.

Not good, he thought, shaking his head. *I need to get these men into the trenches as fast as I can — before the enemy strikes.*

The rain relentlessly pelted down, stinging his face. Once again he scanned the line of men digging. Impatiently, he yelled, "You want to be shot to death before you finish digging your trench? Who taught you to dig?" He watched them struggle to keep the mud from slipping back into the hole. "Shovel faster!"

Further up the line, he noticed a young soldier leaning on his shovel.

Damn, he contemplated to himself. *This kid won't last a day. We'll be sending him back in a box if I don't do something about him.*

25

Shaking his head, he went over and kicked the shovel out from under him, sending the young soldier toppling towards the ground. Mud splattered everywhere.

"You!" he bellowed.

"Yes sir?" Bewildered, the boy scrambled to attention. His eyes were filled with fear as he looked up at his sergeant.

Good. Fear is good, he thought.

"What's your name, boy?"

"Browning, sir." The young boy's thick southern voice shook as he answered. He shuffled his boot back and forth in the mud, gazing at the ground with shame. Mumbling quietly, he added, "Robert Browning...sir." Once again, the young soldier looked at the ground in embarrassment. Slowly, he looked up at Sarge. A small wave of pride showed on his face as he spoke softly. "Like the poet, sir."

An innocent smile overcame Browning's nervousness as he waited for his sergeant's reaction.

Sarge's face softened. Browning's poetry was one of the things that he loved most. Taking his hat off, he wiped his forehead. His heart was pounding as the memories flashed back. "I know the poet well, Private. Now listen up."

The boy's face lit up as he saluted Sarge with respect. "Yes sir!"

Sarge could feel the beads of sweat dripping down his forehead. He hoped that his men thought it was the rain, not sweat. He placed his hat back on his short dark hair. Once again, he became the strict soldier he'd been trained to be.

"Okay, Browning." He paused. Then with a smirk of satisfaction, he added, "Grab that shovel and follow me."

Sarge wanted to make sure the young boy was afraid of him; not so afraid that he wouldn't respond to his orders, but just afraid enough that he wouldn't hesitate when it came time to fight. In fact, he needed all of his men to be that afraid of him. It was the only way they'd survive.

Browning grabbed his shovel and scampered out of the pool of mud that he'd been attempting to deepen. He raced to keep up with Sarge as he walked past the rest of his troop. Stopping abruptly, Sarge turned to face the young boy and barked, "Browning!"

"Yes sir!" Browning almost bumped into his sergeant.

Staring Browning in the eye, he pointed to the ground. "See this spot?"

Browning looked down at the ground, then back at his sergeant. He was unsure about what he wanted. "Yes sir?"

Bending down, Sarge drew a huge "X" on the ground. Then he stood up.

"Dig here," he ordered. "Dig right at this spot here. Dig it deep and wide. And don't stop digging until I tell you to." Sarge looked stern as he belted out the command. "Dig as if your life depended on it. Cuz it does!" And he stormed off.

"Yes sir!" Browning saluted, and started digging like the devil was after him.

Sarge was satisfied that the kid might be okay after all. He wanted to at least make sure that the young boy would last the night. If taking him under his wing was what he had to do, then that's what he'd do. Sarge turned and spat on the ground as if he were making a promise.

He'd make sure that Browning went where he went, stopped when he stopped, breathed when he breathed. He was going to make sure that he never again had to send a telegram home to a mother waiting for her son to return. Yes siree, he was going to make damned sure that this kid lived — and all the other boys in his troop too.

Turning back, he bellowed, "I said dig!"

Browning started to dig harder. He dug into the wetness of the mud. He shoveled until sweat formed on his forehead.

Better, much better, Sarge thought as he headed back down the line to inspect the rest of his men.

Satisfied that they were all digging, he turned back to Browning. In a softer, quieter voice, he commanded, "Okay Browning, you can stop digging now. Jump into that hole and watch for the enemy. Don't want them surprising us today, do we?"

He wanted Browning to know that he was satisfied, but not be so soft that the boy wasn't alert.

Browning looked at his sergeant, "No sir, no surprises. I'll watch really good for you, sir." Jumping into the hole, Browning readied his gun for attack.

"Not for me, Browning. Don't watch for me. Watch for yourself, OK?" Sarge joined him in the hole. Checking his rifle, he added, "You watch your own back. Don't trust anyone else to do that for you." Sarge looked up at Browning. "Not even me. You got it?" Browning didn't reply. Sarge snapped, "I said, you got it?"

"Yes sir. Yes sir! I got you, all right...SIR!"

Sarge could see a small smile on Browning's face. His heart softened toward him. "And you can wipe that smile off your face. This ain't the football game at Jackson High!"

Browning's face dropped. He was serious now. "Yes sir! Sorry, sir!"

Satisfied that Browning was taking him seriously, Sarge pulled his coat closer to his body. A shiver of dampness ran through him as he sunk deep-down into the bowels of the seeping mud.

Inexperienced, he thought to himself. *Signed up to be a hero. Downright shame. Too young to be here.* Sarge shook his head in disgust. *A wannabe! Some hero he'll be if I can't keep him alive.*

Sarge put his hand in his pocket, pulled out a piece of chewing gum, took the wrapper off, and threw the paper into the muddy pool of water that'd collected at his feet. He could feel the numbing of his toes against the wetness of his socks. His boots had leaked, leaving his feet soaking wet.

His thoughts were mixed as his mind wandered. He was worried about his troop. Sarge slumped further down into the hole, wishing it would swallow him up. He'd seen it happen far too often. The young boys that were sent to fight would be changed — scarred for life. There was no glory or victory in war, only ghosts of leftover souls.

"Sarge! Sarge!!"

Snapping back to the current moment, he grabbed his gun and stood up.

"Sarge, Thompson isn't well."

The young voice pierced the fog that'd quickly rolled in.

"What's wrong with him?" Sarge was concerned yet firm.

"He's puking his guts out. Wailing about a bellyache... something about dyin'."

"Thompson, you dying? Hell man, you haven't even been shot at," echoed another voice from the fog.

The men were laughing hard now, slinging remarks around. Sarge knew he needed to act fast, or things would get out of control.

"Thompson!" belted Sarge. "What's going on?"

Thompson's faint voice could be heard down the line. "I think it was the pork in the canteen last night. I'm pukin' my guts out!"

Another voice nearby sarcastically replied, "Couldn't have been all the booze you had, huh?"

Again the men laughed.

"Be quiet!" Sarge snapped. "We aren't here for fun, you

know. The enemy may be sitting out there, listening to us."

The men immediately obeyed him. They respected him and trusted him to keep them safe.

"Oh crap!"

Sarge was getting annoyed at the troop. "What the hell is happening?

"He's puking again."

"Shut up!" Thompson bluntly replied.

Sarge could hear the other men roaring with laughter.

"Go ahead and laugh. It ain't funny."

Sarge was getting fed up. He knew he had to think fast and regain control. Then there was some scrambling and arguing. Sarge tried to see what was happening, but the thickness of the rain and fog made it impossible to make it out.

"What the hell is going on down there now?" Sarge snapped as he started climbing out of the trench.

"Smith is in our foxhole, Sarge. He won't go back to his own."

"Smith, get back where you're supposed to be!"

"But Sarge, it stinks in there."

"I said get back!" Sarge wasn't fooling around now. He was annoyed by these antics.

Smith reluctantly made his way back to his trench. The men quieted down.

"Thompson, you head back to camp, but be careful. We don't want to lose you to the enemy. They could be anywhere. Remember that sniper yesterday? I need a volunteer to help him back."

"I'll go with him, Sarge," Smith wisely offered.

"Okay, Smith, get him back to camp, then wait for my orders. The day is almost done. We should be heading back soon anyway. The rest of you men go about your business, or you'll pay for it when you get back. Is that understood?"

Smith pulled Thompson out of the trench.

"Stay close to the line, and keep your wits about you."

Reassuring himself that they would be okay, Sarge focused on the task at hand.

"Johnson, you crawl back in that hole and keep watch!"

"Do I have to, Sarge?" Johnson whined.

"Johnson!"

"Yes sir!" Johnson made his way back into the trench.

As the men finally calmed down, a satisfied look came over Sarge. It had been a long day, and he was tired. He hadn't slept last night. An angel had appeared to him in a dream, but when she got close to his cot, she transformed into the haggard old woman. She was weeping and pleading with him. She needed an answer, but he didn't have one for her. He'd woken up drenched in sweat and couldn't get back to sleep. Morning had come too fast.

I'm too tired to look after all these inexperienced young boys, he thought to himself as he slipped back into his trench. Pulling his coat tighter around his cold body, he cursed the rain, which was now beating down on him.

Suddenly, he remembered that today was Thanksgiving. He just wanted to be back in his bed, warm and safe. He closed his eyes for a moment and allowed his memories to come gushing back to him.

***

Peter loved teasing Christopher; he liked the way he responded to his mocking. Christopher had a great sense of humor, which he'd brought with him when he moved to New York from the South.

How he loved Christopher. He went and stood behind him, lovingly putting his arms around his waist. Bending down, he nuzzled his neck.

31

"Stop it!" Christopher giggled as he squirmed to free himself. "Your mother will come in and catch us."

"So?" Peter's eyes were dancing with mischief, but his laugh was pure and deep.

"So?" Christopher turned to look at him. "So?" His eyes were growing large with laughter. "So then she'd know our secret."

"Okay, I'll be a good little boy and leave the chef alone in the kitchen. But I'm warning you, if you don't have this turkey on the table in twenty minutes, I'll have to come in here and nibble on you. I'm starving."

***

A single gunshot echoed through the fog. Sarge quickly realized where he was. The rain was still falling hard. Trying to stand up, he shifted his feet against the thickness of the mud that'd accumulated at the base of his boots.

"Where the hell did that come from?" He shouted into the empty silence.

He checked his watch. Twenty minutes had passed. He was relieved. Thompson and Smith should almost be back at camp by now.

The men were mumbling.

"Larson?"

"Here, sir!" The answer emerged from the emptiness.

"Where the hell did that shot come from?"

"Northeast, Sarge."

"Sniper?"

"Could be," came a husky voice from within the fog. "Can't see a damned thing, Sarge. Fog's too thick."

"What should we do?"

This voice was tremoring. His men were scared. *Damn, why did they give me such young kids?* he thought. *Too much responsibility for them.*

"Nothing. Just be alert!" he barked.

There was an uneasy silence. He lowered his gun and stepped back down into the trench.

"Browning?"

"Yes sir?"

He could see the white of Browning's knuckles as he grasped his gun too tightly.

"Keep your eyes open. Both of them."

"Yes sir. Both eyes, sir!"

Browning turned back to the mounted gun that sat atop the mud hole. He was ready for the enemy.

Might be a chance for him after all, thought Sarge.

Again, he scanned the trenches. He needed to make sure that his men were at their posts. The air was thick with anticipation as they waited.

To keep the men alert, Sarge bellowed into the gray dampness of the late afternoon. "Listen up, men! No room for slacking off!"

"Yes, sir," came the unanimous response.

The fog had rolled in even thicker than before. The rain wasn't letting up as the trench slowly filled with water. Sarge's feet were wet and cold.

He thought of his mother. She always fussed over him, making sure that he was dry and warm. He laughed at the memory. It seemed so long ago that his mother had wrapped him in his warm, wool coat and rubber boots. What he would give to be that little boy again. It seemed like it would be a long time until he once again sat at the dinner table eating turkey with his family.

"Not possible today. Sorry, Mom."

"What's that, Sarge?" Browning's face was white with fear.

"Nothing. Go back to your watch." Sarge didn't want to be here. He didn't want to be responsible for these boys, but here he was. There wasn't much he could do about it now.

The heavy rain had made the sides of the trench slippery and uncomfortable to lean against. Sarge tried to wipe the mud off his jacket as it ran down onto his pants and boots.

"Damned rain." Glancing over to the hole next to him, Sarge noticed one of the young men dozing off. "Mackenzie!"

"Yes sir?" Mackenzie sat bolt upright.

"Wake up, or we'll be burying you next!"

"Yes sir!" The young soldier grabbed his gun and positioned it on top of the dirt mound.

After making sure that his order had been taken seriously, Sarge stood very still. He'd learned to smell the enemy. An eerie silence hung over the trench. One of the soldiers shuffled his position, while another pulled out some chewing gum.

Just young boys playing war games. He shook his head again. "Jones! Get over here."

Jones diligently scampered up over the dirt mound and into the trench. "Yes sir!"

Jones was a bright, hefty boy. You usually didn't get both in a kid, but Sarge sensed that Jones had been around the block a few times. He knew how to look after himself.

In a low, swift, clear tone, he ordered, "Take charge of your trench. Keep watch! Grab someone and trade off every thirty minutes. I don't want anyone getting careless today. The men are getting tired and bored. They'll get sloppy if you don't keep them alert."

"Yes sir."

He dismissed the young soldier as rapidly as he'd summoned him. Feeling confident that Jones would make sure every man was alert, he relaxed. Jones was well-liked and respected. They'd listen to him.

He swore under his breath as if he were lecturing himself.

He'd already lost two men in a pointless ambush the week before. That left him with only fourteen in the squad.

Then the other unexpected incident had occurred. The shower. Sarge paused as the memory came rushing back to him. Messy incident.

"Should never have happened," he muttered silently. "Should've seen it coming."

He shuddered as he tried to shake the memory that was pelting his mind. Over and over again, it repeated itself.

Opening his eyes, he briskly made a quick count of his men. He knew how many he'd marched out that morning, but he still counted. Eleven, twelve, and two back at camp. Fourteen all accounted for.

"Damn, I'm getting too paranoid about this stuff." He swore again. He wasn't in a good mood today. The morning sunrise had come too fast. Then there was the five-mile run, hot shower, chow, and drill squad. And now watch duty for the last seven hours.

"Great life!" he snorted, disgusted at the whole situation. Leaning back against the cold, wet wall of mud, he checked his watch. Not long to go before he could pack up the men and head back to base.

"What's that?" asked Browning.

He grumbled, "Just wondering if this lousy rain will ever stop." They both looked at the sky as the black clouds rumbled loudly.

"Not likely," Browning half-laughed. He was starting to like this kid.

Pulling the hood of his raincoat further over his head, he slouched deep down into the hole. He needed some sleep. He was starting to notice how tired he was. He reached for another piece of gum in his pocket.

When his hand touched a piece of notebook paper, he pulled it out. It was his father's handwriting. Warm thoughts filled his head. Since he'd joined the army, not a week had passed without a letter from his father. He'd received the letter at rollcall that morning, but he hadn't had time to read it.

He put his gun down beside him and started reading the letter. But the rain smeared the writing, so he decided to wait until he got back to camp. It was comforting to know that he was loved by his family. All of his father's letters began with a prayer of safety.

Closing his eyes, Sarge took a deep breath. He was homesick.

He knew that all the family would be together today. He could smell the turkey cooking. He could hear all the relatives buzzing around the table, catching up on the news and repeating all the gossip from the last few months.

He could see his mother, a short plump woman who always had a smile on her face. She would be wearing her clean white apron and bringing out the food from the kitchen as she relayed orders to the others.

He could visualize his father. He stood at the head of the table, waiting patiently to say grace. Then he leaned over to cut into the golden-brown turkey, and the juices flowed from the tender white meat. His father was a proud, self-made man. Every year his father would stand at the head of the table, overlooking his flock of children and relatives.

He'd say words that were warm and loving as he gently placed the turkey on each plate, as if it were sacred.

Since Sarge was a little boy, this day had always been a special day in their house. He loved Thanksgiving.

Then he wondered what Catherine looked like now. It'd been a long time since he'd last seen her. Emotions welled up inside him. He swallowed hard, realizing that he missed her. His little girl would be almost eight years old. He winced at the thought. So much time had gone by since everything had happened, but he needed to forget.

Joining the army had helped in the beginning, but now....

His first mission was in South America. Then he signed on for another stint overseas, and now Kosovo.

He could tell from the picture his father had sent him last month that Catherine looked just like Christopher. She was just a little wisp of a thing, with big brown eyes and dark black hair. A pretty pink ribbon was meticulously tied in her hair. He smiled as he thought of his mother's loving hands tying it. Catherine had the same defiant sweetheart chin that Christopher had. No one would be able to resist it.

He looked down at the mud around his boots. His lips pursed tightly as the bitterness seeped in. Catherine was better off without him. She would grow up, go to college, marry someone great, have a family, and live in the suburbs of New York. His father would teach her how to play an instrument, perhaps the harp or violin. His mother would make sure she went to church and joined the right clubs. She would sit with her while she studied at the table at night. Yes, Catherine was better off without him in her life.

An angry sadness passed over him. He missed his family.

The cold of the rain made him shiver. It'd eaten through to his bare skin. Or was it the thoughts of Catherine? Either way, he dismissed them and checked his watch. Grabbing hold of his gun, he shouted to his men.

"Okay men, move out! Be careful. Don't want the enemy to get a trophy today. Let's go back to camp. Then we can get some dry clothes on our backs and some food in our bellies."

He lifted his gun onto his shoulder and motioned for the men to start moving. One by one, the men carefully filed out of the muddy confines of the trench.

One more day over, and I'm still alive, he thought. *Alive, but not living.*

"Come on, Browning." Sarge slapped him on the back. "Last one back buys the beer." With a quick look around him to make sure his men were all out, he heaved himself over the last hump of mud, stood up, and headed back to camp.

CHAPTER 6
THE NEWS

They had a cameraman from the news with our patrol, so I showed them around the neighborhood.

His words appeared on my screen out of nowhere. I smiled. It'd been a few days since I'd heard from my young soldier, so I presumed that he'd moved on with his life. He'd disappeared as quickly as he'd entered my world, and I wondered what the significance of the strange encounter was.

I grabbed the dish towel, wiped my hands, and slipped into the chair in front of my computer.

Hi, welcome back.

Did you see it on the news?

Apparently, he was in a serious mood tonight.

I couldn't remember if there had been anything on TV, but I couldn't recall anything current. How could I tell him that the media was ignoring the war? The story was stale. Kosovo had now been pushed into the corner and left to collect cobwebs. No one cared. Life had moved on.

No, I haven't seen anything about Kosovo.

There was no response.
I prodded carefully so as not to scare him off.

What were they reporting?

They interviewed some of the people.

Because of his mood, I tried to keep it brief.

Good, then it'll be on the news.

He paused. I imagined him replaying the picture in his mind.

Kosovo is supposed to be peaceful now. It wouldn't be politically wise to show that blood is still flowing here.

Silence wrapped itself around me. His feelings were very real. I felt sad for all the soldiers and victims who'd gotten caught up in this political tragedy. But my deepest sadness was for the children who'd bear the unforgivable scars of war.

Breaking the silence, I started typing.

The reality of war....

The words stopped me. I realized that I needed to choose what I said very carefully. His mood could swing at any moment.

The damages are severe. The effect touches everything, from the environment to the physical. But most of all, they cause severely embedded lesions in the mind.

I looked at my words and flinched. These were not the words he wanted to hear from me, so I deleted them.

He was reaching out to someone, anyone, and I happened to be that someone. Even though I was only a name at the other end of the computer, faceless and nonexistent, he needed me. Or at least he needed my words to comfort him through the hell he was living.

The reporters that were here in Kosovo were only from the Armed Forces Network.

I imagined that he was trying to compose himself before he continued.

No one else cares.

I felt his disappointment.

If you don't believe me, go to the news chat rooms. No one wants to talk about Kosovo. They don't want to be bothered.

There was a sharp change in his tone. His mind was back in the present, and he was angry.

I was trying to think of what to say to him. Somehow, he'd acknowledged his anger without clarifying why he was angry. I hesitated. My words had to be right.

Just as I was to about to type, he continued.

No one, except a beautiful lady from Canada.

I smiled. He'd touched my heart. I imagined him recomposing himself, again becoming the tough soldier he was trained to be. But at the same time, he could be very charming. Perhaps he was a good-looking, muscular man with a deep tan. He definitely would be tall and strong, perhaps with dark hair and even darker eyes. Compassionate eyes—yes, definitely compassionate. My soldier would have compassionate eyes, and a few crow's feet and laugh lines. His smile would be enticing, luring, mysterious, and mesmerizing. Of course, it'd be masked by the tough exterior he tried to portray in his words. I wondered how accurate my image of him was.

My smile faded as sadness overtook me. I realized that I would never have the chance to get to know him in person. I'd known that from the beginning, but somewhere during our conversation, I'd let myself think that we would. This exchange was just words on the screen to him, nothing more. I was someone he shared his thoughts with, yet could still hold the prestige of being a tough soldier in his reality.

This was 1999. Skype didn't exist yet, and people didn't frequently ask each other for pictures if they were just chatting online.

Without meeting someone, you can't know what they sound like, but you can feel their tone. Black letters on a white screen, yet they come alive.

Sorry, hard to talk about things. People don't care about Kosovo!

The words were sharp and abrupt. I knew he was backing off, shutting down. Panic took hold of me; I couldn't let him leave. I'd waited too long to talk to him. I grasped at words to keep him online.

I don't know that much about Kosovo. I should've paid more attention to it.

I kept searching my mind for things to say that might trigger an interest in him.

We have so much....

My words drifted. They looked empty, even to me. I couldn't reach him.

Here's the way I see it....

Again, he was a soldier without feelings—a warrior whose heart had turned to stone. I felt sad.

42

The Serbs were the minority, and the Albanians the majority: 10% to 90%. The Albanians wanted an ethnically pure Kosovo, so they tried to run the Serbs out.

I nodded my head in agreement as if he could see me, then laughed to myself. He continued as if I didn't exist, talking to himself and confirming all that'd taken place — like a documentary.

Then in 1989, Milosevic came to power.

There was another short lull.

And all the Albanians had been fired from their jobs.

Silence once again. He was deep in thought. I couldn't begin to imagine the horrific scenes he'd witnessed.

I wanted to type, "I saw a lot of it on the news." But I stopped. I could lie to him, but he'd know.

Actually, there weren't many news stories. Just headlines.

But he was rambling, oblivious to my existence.

They created an all-Serb police force. Then the Albanians rebelled.

But weren't the Serbs the minority?

I was kicking myself for not following the war in Kosovo more closely. I made a mental note to Google the information later, so I could understand the situation better.

My tough soldier rambled on.

So that's when Milosevic cracked down. Started killing everyone.

All the Albanians? I questioned.

He just continued talking as if it'd been pent up inside him for years, and was finally being released.

Then we stepped in. Bombed them into submission and invaded. Now the Albanians are trying to make an ethnically pure Kosovo again, killing all the Serbs, and we....

He paused, deep in thought.

We run around picking up the body parts.

My stomach lurched when I read that sentence. I could see the horror of war through his eyes.

I wanted to stand up and shout to the world, "Haven't previous wars taught us anything? Can't you see that they solve nothing? That they only cause pain and suffering and loss?" But I couldn't because it wasn't my war. It didn't belong to me.

His mind was all over the place.

They don't care. They just want blood. Revenge!

I was starting to understand how he thought. This time, I wasn't worried that I'd lose him. I knew he was just gathering his thoughts before continuing.

If we'd been in the same room, we'd have sipped our coffee quietly, knowing what the other was thinking. Silence would have taken over the moment.

Not long....

He seemed unaware of his surroundings, lost in thought.

It may spread.

The war?

I was getting lost in his spastic ramblings.

This whole Christian/Muslim thing.

He seemed a little surprised that I was having difficulties

following him.

It's a religious war, and we're on the Muslim side. Can you believe that?

How'd that happen?

The Albanians are mostly Muslim. 'To go to Allah.' Very scary.

He was running over the visuals in his mind — the pictures I'd never be able to see.

I went to a Serbian church the other day. It was guarded by a US tank.

He paused.

Now…. Now…. Oh…not now….

I wished that I could be with him, so I could understand what was going through his mind.

Sorry.

I could feel the embarrassment in the apology.

Sorry, a little slow tonight.

I imagined him laughing at the thought of not making sense. He would pull himself up at his desk, straighten his back, and sit at attention like he'd been trained to. Perhaps he'd run his long, calloused fingers through his thick black hair.

Trying to ease his embarrassment, I wrote;

My mind is racing too.

Not the way I usually accomplish things, but it'll do.

I wasn't sure what he meant by that, but it didn't matter to me. All that mattered was that I could be there for him, and that made me feel like I'd eased some of the emotional turmoil he was in.

Got to laugh sometimes.

He was becoming more relaxed with me.

Laughter is important. I'm learning a lot from you.

I sat back and sipped my tea.

Stop teasing.

Putting my tea down, I typed;

I'm serious. I want you to teach me about what's happening.

I've been here about four months. It's not like I haven't been in a war zone before. I was in South America before this, and some other places that I'm not allowed to discuss with anyone. I've seen a lot. He paused. *It's just different this time.*

He'd experienced so much pain in such a short period of time. I thought about how this war must be affecting the other soldiers. I contemplated the young people that had served their country in Vietnam, World War II, and all the other wars. And for the first time in my life, I realized just how emotionally torn they must've been. I considered how their youth had been stolen from them. How many of them would never again be the person they were when they left? It gave me a new understanding of the meaning of war. My heart reached out to them.

You want me to teach you about Kosovo? I don't know if I can.

You know what you feel. That's what I want you to share with me.

46

Only the surface? Not long ago, I gave a box of army food and a hundred marks to an old woman.

There was a long pause.

She could have been my grandmother. Silence. *She asked me, 'What can a bird do to stop the wind?'*

Again he paused. He just needed time to process his thoughts.

I didn't have an answer for her. So I gave her some money and food. But how long will it last? They have no way to get a job.

Why did you join the army?

I couldn't imagine him killing anyone.
After a long pause, he replied.

I was bored? I wanted excitement? It was the thing to do? I don't know; you decide.

Underneath his irony, I knew the real reason had to be deeper. He seemed to be soberly reevaluating.

The truth is…I was running away from something.

From what?

I guess I got away, but now I'm tired… So very, very tired.

Although I was curious about what he was running away from, I knew that I would have to wait for the answer.

Mentally tired? Emotionally tired? You have too much heart to be in the army.

Both. I should be an English teacher. Make a difference, you know. I was studying…night school. I was doing well too. I had everything I wanted. Then in the blink of an eye, it all changed. But you wouldn't understand.

Understand what?

Nothing. Forget I said anything. I shouldn't have mentioned it.

The long silence was awkward.

Without heart, you can't be in the army. These nineteen-year-old kids pick up pieces of old ladies and children, and put them in bags. Big, black garbage bags.

Oh my god. I felt sick at the thought of what I'd just heard. He wanted to shock me—maybe even hurt me a little. And he had. I tried to get the images out of my mind, and I figured that he was trying to forget the images that tore at him too.

Sorry, didn't mean to say that. Just forget it, okay?

His words drifted off.

Too much, he added, as if that confirmed the statement.

I didn't want to pressure him. I frantically grasped at my words. "Careful now," I cautioned myself. "Go easy on him. You're losing him again."

Will you talk about something else for a while?

So I changed the subject.

I feel so helpless and spoiled here in Canada. Can I do something to help the Serbs?

As selfish as it sounds, I needed to say that.

What can you do?

It was more of a defeated statement than a question.

48

That's what the old lady said to me the other day, and I had no answers.

He was hurting. I could sense it, feel it, and almost touch it.

We sat in silence. I'd felt the despair in his words. And in my mind, I could hear the old woman's defeated voice. I could almost see her malnourished, frail body. I felt the words strike my heart with a sympathy and compassion that I'd never experienced before. Hot tears uncontrollably trickled down my cheeks.

How old is she?

Eighty or so. But then I'm told that war can age a person, so their real age can't always be determined.

And her family?

I wanted to share the experience with him. I wasn't sure, but I longed to know. I thought of my mother and father and how much they meant to me.

Not sure. They all care for each other as best they can. He sounded exhausted. *They all become a family.* He paused. *Listen, this is too much for tonight.*

I was caught off-guard by his words, but I wanted to be able to visualize it.

They stick together?

I didn't want to hurt him, but something inside me needed to know. I needed him to allow me to feel his pain. Maybe I thought I could ease it a little if I felt it. I had this notion that I might be able to take away some of the burden he was carrying in his heart. I didn't know what to do; I just knew I didn't want him to feel this way anymore.

His next words stood out on the screen, and the pain gushed in.

I'm hurting myself by getting involved.

I felt the anguish of his suffering as the tears trickled down my face like a river.

I began to cry for him, for the old women, and for all the people who'd gotten caught in fate's hand. Cry for the children who'd been robbed of their lives, for the mothers who would never hear their babies' voices again, for the grandparents, the brothers, the sisters. Yes, I needed to cry.

We didn't need words to feel each other's emotions. We'd connected as two souls in the dark, reaching out to each other. We'd become one through the pain.

I realized I couldn't leave my soldier in this state of mind. I needed to leave him with a happy memory — not the haunting ones that were eating away inside of him. My mind raced vividly, trying to grasp at a topic that would achieve that goal.

Do you have a girlfriend?

I thought perhaps that would be a safe subject — a lead-in to something a little more cheerful.

Can you imagine how it feels to have five old women look you in the eye, and tell you they have no hope?

He was rambling again. The emotional turmoil that was gushing through his mind was enormous.

I'd poured salt in his wound. We were individuals with different backgrounds and thoughts. He'd entered my world and brought his inner feelings with him. And I'd taken on the colors of his pain and suffering.

I swallowed hard to rid myself of the dryness that was closing my throat.

Tell me how it felt.

I'm not sure.

What he said next surprised me.

I wanted to run away. It seems like I'm always running away.

I imagined him fighting the need to cry. I wasn't expecting that answer from a tough American soldier. Now he was a little boy — scared, confused, and craving the safe sanctuary of his mother's arms.

At that moment we seemed to have created a level of communication without words. A world away from each other, and yet within an arm's reach. I knew he was crying for those he couldn't save. For those whose suffering he couldn't stop. And I was crying for the youth that he'd lost.

They say that if you look at a dead person, you can see their soul. That when a person dies, their soul leaves their body. But if you can still see their soul, does that mean that we're so lost in this wretched war that even our souls can't rest?

I had no answer for him. Sometimes one wonders if the weeping is more out of fear for ourselves than sympathy for the dead. At this moment, I wasn't sure who I was weeping for.

I don't know. Can you?

I've read that when we stand on the border of reality, we're afraid that we'll lose our identities if we plunge in. But this fear was different. It was from the pit of his heart and soul. He carried a fear deeper than I would ever experience.

I don't have any real answers for them.

I'd opened Pandora's Box, and I needed to leave it alone. I softened my feelings and typed on the screen as if he could hear me speaking.

I'm here for you.

CHAPTER 7
THE REFUGE

He was here again, filling my home with emotions so deep that the walls seemed to be closing in on me.

The media told me that nothing had really changed. The rich are still rich, and the poor are still poor. I told them I was poor.

I was taken aback by this remark.

Are you?

Yes, I am. By American standards. But we're so rich, compared to other countries. I'm the first in my family to finish high school, let alone college.

I envisioned that he was pondering.

Can you see me as a teacher? Stupid idea, huh?

I don't think so. Teaching can be very rewarding.

Yeah, maybe if you're teaching rich kids. Not many kids graduate where I come from. Too many gangs. And now I'm here. What chance do kids have here? He paused. *I guess I can't be that stupid if I'm still*

53

alive.

Now I was getting worried about him. He seemed so depressed.

Okay, we're getting far too serious now.

My father worked long hours to keep the family above water. And Ma would work in the factory, came home, clean the house, and make dinner. And she still found time to make sure we did our studies. She sat with us at the kitchen table every night. She tried to help us, but after a while, it became too hard for her. She never got much of an education because she had to work at such a young age. You did that in those days if you came from a poor family.

You know what she did when she got us all settled in bed? She mended and ironed for rich people. Sometimes I would get up in the middle of the night to get a drink of water, and there she'd be, humming and mending. Then she'd get up the next day and work in the factory.

I'd never stopped to think about people who came from nothing. I felt compassion toward his mother—a strong, loving woman.

She'd spot me and scold me, but then she'd go into the kitchen and get me a cookie. She'd hug me and tell me not to tell my sisters. I'd run off and eat the cookie in the darkness of my bedroom. She always made me feel special. My father was a good man too. He wanted me to go to college and get a degree. Make something of myself. He was so proud of me when I finally started. He was like a peacock spreading his feathers, telling everyone that his son was in college.

I believed that his father was a good man. He'd brought up his son to have compassion and respect for life. How could anyone not be a good man who wanted these things for their child?

Then everything changed. It all changed. He hesitated. *Sorry, I think I need to go.*

It was as if he'd just realized how much he'd said to me, and how deep he had let me into his thoughts. He seemed embarrassed.

What changed?

He didn't answer.

Please don't go yet.

I wanted to put my hand on his arm.

That brought up too many feelings. They're feelings I don't need right now, so I've been avoiding them.

There was an awkward silence.
Curiosity pulled at me, but my desire to help him mend his hurt was stronger.

Let me try to help you. It'll make you feel better.

I've pushed them down. Too deep.

It was as if he'd just realized that those feelings actually existed. I didn't want him to leave hurting and sad, so I talked quickly to keep his attention. I wanted to get through to him and break the barrier of despondency.

How about if I tell you about where I grew up? You'd love it there.

I waited for his response. There was a long silence. I thought that he might've logged off, but after several minutes, he answered.

Okay, go ahead.

I didn't think he was really interested. But at the same time, I was relieved that I'd be able to give him some small part of me—a particle of hope. A dream he could lose himself in. I imagined him leaning back in his chair, smirking at the thought of a stranger wanting to tell him a fairytale. I smiled.

I'm a good storyteller. I've been told that for years. I started to describe the place where I grew up. For the first time, I realized just how lucky I was to have grown up in such freedom and beauty. I'd always appreciated it, but not with the intensity that I was feeling that night.

When I describe my birthplace to you, it'll leave you with a dream to return to when you need to escape reality. A place without pain and suffering. This place will be your dream to hold onto, whenever you need to escape.

He didn't answer. I hoped that he'd allowed his mind to wander back through time, to a moment when he had a dream, an ambition, or a cherished thought of hope.

Okay, you sit back now and rest, while I tell you about it. I grew up on a small gulf island on the Pacific Ocean. It's called Denman Island, which means 'gem of the sea.' It's God's country.

I waited for him to respond.

Go ahead, he finally encouraged. He was focused, and I was relieved.

It's full of tall fir trees. Under them, there's a carpet of lush, green, velvet grass. Ten acres of land and beauty. Land like you'll never be able to see again. Precious land. Now we're going to walk up the driveway to the pond together.

I felt like I was telling a story to a traumatized child—trying to calm him down, and gently wiping away his tears with my words. I imagined that I was sitting beside him, tightly holding his hand, gently stroking his head, and softly soothing his fears.

See how beautiful it is? Close your eyes, and imagine being there. Smell the essence of the sea. Listen to the breeze as it whispers through the tall, white elm trees. Hear it sing in a rhythmic pattern – a song of joy that's deep and happy. Let's go and sit by the pond over there. See that bench? Come and sit with me. Relax, close your eyes, and breathe in the beauty that's embracing your soul. Let nature take your heart away.

Although I couldn't touch him or see him, I could feel the calm embracing him. I continued.

Look within your mind. Let it focus on things that're beautiful. Can you see the mother mallard duck and her little ducklings? I love to sit here and watch them swim. Mama duck is being protective. She comes here every year to have her babies because she knows they'll be safe here. She's teaching them the ways of nature, so they can become strong and survive. Can you feel it? Can you reach your hand out? Touch the beauty?

At that moment, my heart swelled with love.

There're bull rushes on the pond. See all the vibrant yellow daffodils? My father planted hundreds of daffodils here. He loves flowers. Can you see them nodding their golden heads in the gentleness of the breeze? It's springtime. Smell the strong essence of the snowdrops. How fragile, pure, and white they look. Yet how strong they must be to survive the long, cold winters and become the most sensual spring flowers.

Shhhh.... I put my finger up to my lips. Listen. Hear the birds singing in harmony like the music of a concerto. They are busy building nests and having families. It's such a happy time.

Look up. There's a blue heron. Can you see her, way up in the tall fir tree? See her nest? She only has one baby a year, but she's such a proud mama. She brings her babies to the beach in front of our house and struts around.

I paused a moment.

Close your eyes and listen. What do you hear? Can you hear the seagulls crying? They're playing a game of tag, calling out to each other as they swoop and climb. Shhhh....

I continued in a low whisper as I spoke the words out loud.

See the little brown squirrel scampering up the tree over there? Now he's sitting on the branch laughing at us, ever so cheekily. He's nattering to us. Can you hear him?"

Yes, I think I can, the soldier typed.

My heart skipped a beat as I saw his words on the screen. In that moment, I knew I'd touched him and brought some calm into his life. I knew this refuge would stay with him forever, and he'd take it out whenever he needed one. It could be a hiding place from reality. I was excited that I had the ability to make him dream. More than ever, I wanted to make him happy — to feel the deep love, beauty, and serenity that embraces us.

Close your eyes. See it. Feel it. Live it. I paused. *My brave soldier, life is beautiful.*

At that very moment, I sincerely meant every word I said. I was so grateful to be alive.

See the buds on the trees?

I wish you could whisper this to me as I fall asleep. It's very soothing.

Oh, how I wish I could too. More than anything in my heart, I wish I could too.

It's like I can hear your voice talking to me. Strange, isn't it?

Yes, very strange.

Neither of us said anything for a moment.

But you can replay this dream whenever you need it. All you have to do is reach into your heart and bring it out, even if only for a moment. It's your dream, and it's my gift to you.

I quickly continued, so I wouldn't lose my momentum.

Lie back, so the sun kisses your face. Let the breeze whisper to you. We are so lucky to experience this beauty. So very, very, lucky.

I had tears of joy welling up in my eyes.

Why do you waste such beauty on me?

The words were like a slap on the face. I felt my dream disappear, and a feeling of unworthiness surfaced.

I'm sharing with you as you've shared with me.

I wanted him to know I was hurt.

Why? he asked coldly.

Because you have a heart.

We all do. His answer came sharply and quickly.

No, I snapped back at him. *Not everyone.*

I paused for a brief moment, and collected myself. Then to confirm what I meant, I added,

People have hearts, but they don't feel with them. You have the ability to see into the reality of the situation.

It takes a lot to build a shell hard enough to survive. But I'm not sure it's good to make cracks in it.

It's okay. I'll bring the crazy glue.

I hoped he would laugh at my joke.

Cute.

It was a sarcastic answer, but I could feel the tension easing within him.

If this is too much for you, I'll understand. I know you have to be tough to survive.

I didn't want to make him soft, so he'd make a mistake. I couldn't be responsible for a tragedy.

I think I need to get some sleep.

Okay.

I'm not sure.

It took me a minute to realize that he was referring to my previous statement.

I'm truly sorry if I upset you. I didn't mean to—

I feel like throwing up when I get on a roll.

I felt terrible for making him relive such agony. I didn't know what else to say, so I just said,

I'm so sorry.

But I'm not sure how I'll feel in the morning.

I won't bother you again. If you need to talk, I'll be here. I'll let you

get in touch with me.

The guilt that ran through me was tremendous. I felt so selfish, making him relay feelings that were buried. Now I'd once again brought them to the surface.

No! I think it's good. But it worried me that my feelings were so strong. I didn't even know they were that significant. I can't be the big bad Sarge if I'm walking around crying. In a playful yet serious way, he added, *Not good for the image.*

I wanted to say, "To hell with the image. Look at your feelings, the way you hurt." I wanted to write the president or the prime minister and say, "For God's sake, can't anyone do something for these men?"

But I knew I couldn't compromise his confidentiality. This conversation was meant to be just between the two of us.

I think I need you more than you know.

His answer was more than I'd hoped for.

If not for you, I might've ended up like the kid that shot himself in the bathroom the other day.

My heart sank as I read those words.

Oh, stop worrying, my friend. I don't have those thoughts. I just didn't know I had such strong feelings.

Is that good or bad?

I held my breath.

They kind of scare this 192-pound man. Not sure.

Because society requires that soldiers remain detached?

I was starting to get angry again, but I knew I had no right to say anything.

If I walk around crying all day….

You won't! You'll be just fine.

Still, I might not get back on your couch.

My couch?

Yes, at least not for therapy.

He was teasing me, and I felt a lot better. I giggled to myself.

Okay, that's fair.

See, I'm back to normal again.

He'd realized his emotional state, and that was a good sign.

Yes, your humor is back. I like that.

I hoped he would sense my smile through my words.

Well, I'm tired, and I have to be up in three hours. I need to get to bed.

Yes, I can sense that. Thank you for sharing your feelings with me. Remember, if you need me, I'm here.

That's comforting to know. But I think my bill for counseling will be tremendous.

I liked the light, joking side of my soldier. It was good to feel him laughing.

This one's on the house.

And with that, I bid him goodnight.

Chapter 8
THE LOST LOVE

A candle gently flickered against the thin-paned window, leaving ghosts dancing on the wall of darkness. In the background, "America the Beautiful" was quietly playing on the radio in one of the tin-roofed huts. Dark shadows pulled at his heart as he silently stood in the ebony of night.

He headed to the nightstand beside the bed. Opening the drawer, he pulled out a bottle of whiskey, removed the cap, and took a huge gulp. The whiskey burned as it slid down his throat. Taking another gulp, he put the lid back on and placed it back into the drawer.

He reached into his coat pocket and pulled out a tattered photo. A smile formed in the corners of his lips. Mixed emotions enveloped him, and his mind raced back to forgotten times. In this frenzy, he stumbled out of the front door into the darkness.

Memories burned into every inch of his body like the hot, smoldering flow of lava. In the hollow of the night, his voice cried out in pain, "Christopher!"

He yearned for the days of youth and discovery, remembering the times when he sweetly rested his head in Christopher's lap.

He longed for the times when the beauty of poetry softly flowed from the innocence of his sweet lips. He wanted to return to the moment when Christopher reached out and cupped his face with his slender hands. When their souls spoke so clearly, yet a word never escaped their lips. When innocence prevailed in their untouched world.

He felt dead and forgotten by the human race. Devoid of a visible tear, he asked himself, "Where do I belong?"

He wanted to cry for the forbidden desires of tomorrow, and the demolished dreams of yesterday.

He was a child lost amid a galaxy of stars, and Christopher was the heavenly body that awakened his heart. He gave him breath when he couldn't go on, and eyes to see when he was blind. Christopher was the breeze that gently whispered to him in the night, and the stranger that danced in the twilight of happiness. He was his reality.

Everything beautiful that awakened within Peter belonged to him. All the goodness that Peter craved was his to share—the oneness of heart and the purity of soul. Christopher was his whole world, his everything.

But tonight, that seemed like another lifetime. The last time he'd felt like Peter was the last time Christopher called him by that name.

Now that Christopher was gone, this nameless existence had stripped him of his identity. Raising his face to the stars, he felt his heart being ripped from his chest.

But now that he'd met this stranger, maybe telling her about what happened could give him back his identity. Maybe, just maybe, he could be Peter again.

"Where are you tonight?" He moaned in agony like an animal that'd lost its limbs. "Where are you now that I need to feel the strength of your heart beating rapidly against mine?" He looked into the void of night. "Oh, this blackness that swallows me!"

His hands grasped the railing in front of him to steady the faintness that washed over him. With whitened knuckles, he cried out into the barren darkness.

"Christopher!"

It was an eerie, screeching sound that sent animals in the forest running to the safety of their homes, until all that was left was the sound of his heart being ripped from the deepest of dungeons. The sound echoed in the emptiness. His heart had been twisted with the pain of memories, and suffocated by the dreams of reality.

Once again he looked at the gorgeous man in the photo. He had kept Christopher close to his heart for so long. A helpless sigh escaped his lips as he placed the photo back in his coat pocket.

Flicking his cigarette into the darkness, he watched the red ember land on the ground a few feet in front of him.

Without emotion, he pulled his coat collar closer around his neck, masking the cold night that inaudibly clutched at him. He felt the presence of the man he'd loved so deeply — his quiet presence and the depth of their dreams. So many beautiful thoughts entwined in the memories of his mind, and yet emptiness encased him. Quietly, he turned and walked back toward the tin-roofed hut.

The night was silent in his presence. Innocence had long left him, and in its place, the black feeling of despair lurked in the empty corners of his heart.

CHAPTER 9
THE REFLECTION

The conversations with my soldier had become more infrequent. The vivid reflections of our sharing of events pulled even more endlessly at me. My thoughts and feelings about him repeatedly crept into my dreams.

"These nightmares have to stop!" I gasped as I sat up in bed, trying to catch my breath. Sweat rolled down my back. The room was dark, and only a reflection of the moon danced on the walls. I wiped my forehead on my nightshirt. Glancing at the clock, the green digits said three o'clock.

The old woman kept appearing in my dreams. She was very vivid and real. I felt her presence enveloping me, trying to become part of me. Her mouth was taut and drawn, her eyes hollow and haunting. Again and again she returned, always the same dream. I shivered at how realistic her presence was. I couldn't get her voice out of my mind; it was weak and sad, almost a whisper. Her words echoed throughout the blackness of my subconscious.

"What can a bird do to stop the wind?"

She held her hand out, reaching for the miracle that no one could provide. I tried to shake the vision of the dream. I could feel my heart uncontrollably pounding under my nightshirt.

Sleep didn't come after the dream; it never did. I tried to close my eyes, but my thoughts wouldn't allow me to escape.

"A cup of tea might help sooth my mind."

Slipping out of bed, I headed for the kitchen. Picking up the kettle, I walked over to the sink. I wondered what my soldier was doing at that moment. Once again, my thoughts lapsed back to the old woman, and a chill ran down my spine.

Turning on the faucet, I placed the kettle under the spout and thought about the people of Kosovo. "How do they manage without water?" Suddenly, I was aware of every luxury in my life.

I placed the kettle on the stove and started to reach over to turn it on, then stopped. Would the refugees of Kosovo be sitting around the fire, warming their hands right now? Did they miss their hot cups of tea around the table with their families, laughing and sharing stories about days gone by? I turned the knob on high, scolding myself. "There's nothing you can do for them; it's just the way it has to be. You have to let this go."

Gazing out my window into the night, I remembered how beautiful Denman was. Stars circled the bright yellow moon; it looked like a well-practiced ballet. Diamonds twinkled on the glass surface of the deep-blue ocean. Large elm trees swayed slowly in the breeze, conducting a quiet melody with their rustling leaves, and crickets and frogs provided accompaniment. I loved living on Denman Island. I'd grown up there, and its beauty was interwoven with my heart.

I was so engrossed in my thoughts that I jumped when the kettle whistled.

"Now, stop this at once," I reprimanded myself out loud. "You're being ridiculous!"

I was upset that I hadn't heard from my soldier for a while, and I thought that was why I was thinking about the old woman.

The big easy chair looked inviting as I walked into the front room. Slumping down into it, I curled my cold feet up under me. Perhaps reading would help me settle down. Concentration wasn't going to be easy; my mind was still in Kosovo with the old woman and my young soldier. After reading the same paragraph several times, I decided it was useless to even try. So I lowered the book onto my lap and sat back, allowing my thoughts to run free.

Strains of the young soldier's words etched vivid pictures in my mind. I imagined that his shoulders were slumped and defeated.

I reached for my tea. Sipping it carefully, I felt the hot liquid on my lips. I swallowed hard, convincing myself that the reason why my throat was tight and dry was because I was coming down with something. But I knew it wasn't true.

Outside my window, the sun was rising. I could see the morning rays peeking through the large maple trees. The hills were draped in vibrant jewel-tones: gold, orange, and crimson. The emerging of fall was well underway, and the changes were breathtaking. The mist was lifting under the warmth of the morning sun.

I wanted to share my feelings with my soldier. It wasn't the first time I'd written to him. Over the last few weeks I'd written many emails, but I hadn't heard anything back. Nevertheless, I didn't give up and kept writing him. My hope was that one day I'd sit at my computer, and his words would pop up at me like they used to.

My Dear Brave Soldier,

With the following words, I hope I will be able to bring you a small ray of happiness. Today, I will carry you in my thoughts and give you my strength.

May God watch over you.

I paused, surprised at the words that had come tumbling out. I wasn't a religious person, but at that moment, I truly believed that God would watch over him. I continued.

It saddens me to think of the hurt you carry in your heart. My thoughts are with you during this dark period of your life. If I can bring but a moment of happiness to you, then I'd like to try.

This morning, I sat in my house and watched the sun rise. You were in my thoughts, and I wanted to share what I saw.

I'm sending you a letter that I hope will bring a smile to your face, and a wish that you'll feel better when the darkness smothers you. Always remember that today will pass, and tomorrow will bring a new dawn.

You were right when you said that I couldn't begin to understand what you're going through. And I can't see what your eyes see, or feel what your heart feels. I can only imagine. What I do know is that my heart reaches out to you, to all the other young soldiers, and to the victims of Kosovo.

Sincerely….

I looked at the computer screen. We'd never exchanged names. I'd always called him my young soldier, but I'd never told him my name. I actually knew very little about him, but at the same time, I knew more about him than my next-door neighbor might know about me in his lifetime. He'd shared his most vulnerable thoughts and secrets with me, yet he was just an avatar.

I mused at the concept of modern technology. How advanced it was, but it was still so lacking. Perhaps we weren't meant to know names and hair colors. Perhaps this exchange was just a crossing of paths that was just meant to give each other something that was special and sincere, and nothing more.

I decided to change my closing.

Holding you close to my heart….

Then I quickly added one of my short writings that I thought he'd enjoy.

How beautiful is the gift of autumn. Mother Nature is so busy running around with her pallet of paints, splashing all within her sight, creating a masterpiece for all to see. The maple and oak trees are dressed in their finest attire, standing so regally in the silhouette of the coming night. They know this stage in their life is but for a short period, so they appreciate every second they have. They know it's not the end of a season, but the beginning of wintertime. As we all must in our own lives, they stop and rest. They slow down. They think about the seasons we experience, and prepare for the coming of spring.

Thus, it's a new beginning. The continuing cycle starts again. Everything nature creates returns taller, stronger, and more vibrant. In the beginning, the oak stands timid and small among the other great creations. And as each season passes, it grows continually, reaching until it gets stronger and steadier. Then at last, it can stand by itself against the winds of life.

Each season allows nature to add the finishing touches. In her most elegant of manners, Mother Nature returns, until the mighty oak can stand tall and strong.

Place your hand in front of your mouth, and feel the breath you breathe. Be thankful for the privilege of being alive. Stop and appreciate the beauty of life, but also know that it's not the loss of breath, the falling of leaves, or even the bending of branches that's important.

It's knowing that after this precious breath, there's another and yet another. Each one is just as precious, if not more, than the one before. With each breath we breathe, and with each leaf that falls, a new breath and a new leaf replaces them. We're given the chance to experience an even more beautiful, deeper meaning of life. We are the fortunate few who've been given the gift of seeing the beauty within the world, and the heart within the soul. We truly are blessed!

Happy with what I'd written, I quickly sent the email off and hoped that my soldier would read it before he went to bed. I was feeling much better now. Glancing at the clock on the wall, it was time to get ready for work. I knew today would be a beautiful day.

It turned out that work went slowly, and it was difficult to concentrate. My mind kept wandering back to my soldier and the people of Kosovo. I hadn't accomplished much in the office, and I scolded myself as I started to put the paperwork away. In another twenty minutes, I'd be able to shut down the office and head home. I was wondering if my soldier would come back. I was beginning to worry that I'd never hear from him again. Finishing off the little things that I needed to do, I forwarded the phones, locked the doors, and headed home.

Once home, I went to my computer and checked my email. Nothing. The next few hours were filled with playing a game of solitaire, writing my friends, and surfing the web. In my heart, I was hoping that my young soldier would appear online. By ten, I'd accepted the fact that he wasn't going to show once again. As hard as I tried, I couldn't shake off the disappointment I felt. I felt a wave of sadness. I'd grown very close to this young stranger.

As I turned out the light, I whispered softly, *"Good night, my young soldier, wherever you are. May you always be safe."*

71

CHAPTER 10
THE STREAM

As the sun beat down on the forgotten world of Kosovo, the stream was cool and calming that morning. He just needed to get away from all the ghosts of war. His life had become too demanding. He was starting to lose sight of who he was—not only the way other people perceived him, but also who he truly was.

So today, he'd be himself. He'd take this time to think and feel. He needed to get in touch with the feelings that'd been locked deep inside of him, hidden from the outside world. These were the very emotions that the online stranger had opened up. Today, he needed to be *real*.

He sat down on the small patch of lush green grass near the edge of the river, and stared across at the forest on the other side of the bank. It was simplicity in all its beauty. He bent his head back and lifted his face to the sun, soaking in the warmth it emitted. Closing his eyes, he allowed himself to drift into an area of his being where he felt happy and safe.

The river gurgled as it slowly wound its way along the mud-like banks that'd been carefully etched out of sharp rocks and sand. Familiar with the security of its boundaries, the bubbling river carefully flowed over and around the boulders and fallen debris that tried to mar its slow, methodical journey to the sea.

The sound soothed the young soldier. It brought back memories from the past, which held a precious place in his heart. The breeze lifted the coolness from the water, and mingled it with the warmth of the sun's rays. It softly caressed his face with all the tenderness that held purity sacred. Like an abandoned animal, he felt a loneliness gush over him—a deep, sorrowful loneliness that he'd tried hard to forget. Memories flowed like a broken dam as he sat quietly on the river's edge.

One by one, the leaves slowly fell from the trees onto the ground. They wove a blanket of color into a carefully designed quilt.

To the right, he saw a squirrel scampering along an old fallen log, stopping only briefly to observe the man that sat watching him. He smiled as he remembered the story the stranger had painted for him—the pond, the ducks, and the squirrel. He watched in silence, amused at how the squirrel reacted just as she'd conveyed in the story.

The squirrel scurried across the moss-covered ground as he gathered winter supplies to feed his family. At that moment, the soldier felt happy. The stories the online stranger had told him were becoming an important part of his survival in Kosovo. When things seemed too overwhelming, he'd close his eyes and imagine her voice. When life was a dark abyss of overwhelming emotions, he'd allow himself to feel the tenderness and awe of her stories. Then his heart would stop hurting, if only for the moment.

But it did stop, and that was what was important to him. All the blood and gore would ease, and the wounds that pierced his heart would slowly close. Once again, he'd be able to breathe.

73

He took a deep breath and released it. As he inhaled, he let in all the people that loved and cared about him, and as he exhaled, he let the dark demons escape from his soul. At this moment, he felt safe. Lying there on the grass, he allowed himself the luxury of remembering.

***

Peter was twelve when Christopher moved into the neighborhood. Christopher was two years younger than him. It was a Saturday morning, and Peter was running late for his music lesson.

"If you don't get going now, you'll miss it completely," Peter's mother rebuked as she pushed his violin case into his hand. "Your father works hard to pay for your lessons."

How many times had he heard her say that? He hated it when she lectured him. He hated the violin, hated how it sounded, and hated learning it.

"Why can't I play the saxophone, Ma?" Peter whined as she did up his jacket, making sure he was warm and dry. He fidgeted. When she was finished, he mimed playing the saxophone.

His mother tutted with disgust. "Only fly-by-night musicians play the saxophone. Not the violin. Now that's a beautiful instrument."

He squirmed as she slicked down his unruly hair with her hand. He reached up and pushed her hand away.

"Ma, I'm not a baby!"

"Well, I always have to keep reminding you to do things like zip up your jacket. Then you get a cold, and I end up having to take time off work to look after you."

Peter fidgeted again, trying to work the zipper himself. His mother reached down to help him, but he turned away.

"I hate the violin!"

"And I hate working, but do you see me quitting my job?"

She always had a reply. He picked up his violin case and headed toward the door. Stepping just out of her reach, he snapped, "I'm going to be late."

His mother shook her head. All her children were growing up too fast.

"Remember to stop by Mr. Baker's shop and bring me a dozen eggs on your way."

"Yes, Ma," he absentmindedly answered, not really paying attention to her instructions.

"You have the money in your pocket." She paused. "Don't forget."

"I won't," Peter said, a little too sarcastically.

"And don't break them. Last time, you cracked two before you got them home."

Escaping out the door, Peter sighed. He was relieved that he was away from her.

As he headed down the street, he spotted a little boy sitting on the cement steps of Mrs. Swede's house. *He must be the new kid that everyone's talking about*, he thought to himself. *Mrs. Swede said his name was Christopher.*

His mother and Mrs. Swede had grown up together in this neighborhood. They had gone to school together and worked in the same factory. Everyone liked Mrs. Swede; she was always nice, friendly, and caring.

Christopher was a tiny boy with an air of sadness. Peter stared at Christopher as he walked closer. There was something about Christopher that made him realize that he was going to like him.

Peter slowed his pace, trying to get a closer look without being conspicuous about it. For weeks prior to Christopher moving in, he'd overheard all his neighbors talking. At the market, a group of women were talking about how Christopher's parents had been killed in a car accident. They called him "a poor little orphan boy."

Apparently, Christopher's mother was Mrs. Swede's youngest sister. They'd had a falling-out when they were younger, and hadn't talked for twelve years. Mrs. Swede didn't even know that her sister was married, much less had a baby. It wasn't until that scary social worker in his black sedan with the tinted windows came knocking on her door that she learned that the little boy had nowhere to go. Finally, after the social worker visited her several times, Mrs. Swede agreed to take him in.

He'd overheard one woman saying, "Poor child. Nobody wanted him. Had nowhere else to go, no relatives except Mrs. Swede. No money left to her. The father drank it all away—a good-for-nothing, if you know what I mean. He's lucky that Mrs. Swede has a kind heart."

So there Peter stood, staring at Christopher. *He doesn't look the way they described*, he thought. He wanted to say hello, but the words didn't come. He felt awkward and embarrassed. Some twelve-year-olds get that way when they suddenly realize the feelings they have. As Peter got closer to him, Christopher tried to hide his red eyes by looking down at the pavement. But he knew he'd been crying.

Finally, a single syllable emerged from Peter's mouth. "Hi."

Shyly, Christopher looked up at him. "Hi."

"You're the new kid everyone's talking about, aren't you?"

Christopher didn't answer right away. Instead, he kept looking at the ground. Peter thought he was going to cry again.

"What's wrong with your face?"

"Nothing," Christopher said quietly as he slightly turned away from him.

"You been crying?" Peter moved closer to Christopher, examining his face.

"No!" Christopher dropped his head down so he couldn't see his eyes.

"Really?" Peter stepped closer, trying to see for himself. "Looks to me like you were crying."

"How is that any of your business?" Christopher snapped, growing impatient with his questions.

Quickly, Peter stepped back from him. Christopher was angry, and Peter didn't want to be in his way when he exploded. He'd learned that much about upset people from his older sisters. Whenever he put his nose where it didn't belong, they quickly snapped it off. He'd learned to stay out of their way when they were crying or in a bad mood. That's for sure! People could be unpredictable—happy one minute, crying the next.

"Geez, what's the big deal?"

Examining him more closely, Peter realized how tiny and delicate Christopher was. So vulnerable. He wanted to say something nice to him. He didn't mean to hurt Christopher's feelings. He just wanted to talk to him, but the words were coming out all wrong. So he opted to keep it simple.

"Why are you mad at me?"

Christopher shifted his position, ignoring him. So he took a few steps and bent down to look at him.

"Did you get in trouble or something?" Peter inquired. Christopher started to stand up.

"Don't leave," Peter quickly said.

"Why should I stay?" Christopher defiantly, but just slightly, lifted his heart-shaped chin.

"Look, I didn't mean to hurt your feelings. I'm not good at this sort of thing. I mean, I have two sisters, and I know they cry. That's all. It's what some people do when they're upset. Isn't it?" Christopher didn't answer, so he kept talking. "Want to talk about it?"

Christopher's face mellowed, and he sat back down.

Peter had heard his Ma ask all his sisters that question when they'd been crying about something or other. It seemed to make them feel better. He wasn't sure how; he just knew they stopped crying. They seemed to be the magic words.

"Nope." Still looking down at the steps, Christopher nervously played with a loose button on his yellow shirt. Peter thought about how gorgeous Christopher looked. Most people didn't look good in yellow, but it really set off his features.

Christopher's appearance struck him hard—both his outer and inner beauty.

"Are you crying about your parents?"

Peter looked at his violin case, then back at Christopher. He knew he was going to be in trouble if he was late for his lesson, but for some reason, it just didn't seem important anymore. He sat down beside Christopher on the cement step, then gently placed his violin case beside him.

Christopher swallowed hard, trying to stop the sobs that were forming in his throat.

"Bet it hurts real big, huh?"

Christopher dug into the pocket of the yellow shirt he was wearing. He was trying find a handkerchief, but he didn't have one. Quickly, Peter quickly reached into his pocket and pulled out the clean handkerchief his mother had put in there. It was rumpled, so he tried to straighten it out before he handed it to Christopher.

"Just in case," Ma would tell him. He'd never understood what she meant until that moment. He smiled and silently thanked his mother for her thoughtfulness. Then he made a mental note to never go anywhere without a clean hankie again.

"Here, use mine." Christopher looked up at him, took it, and began wiping the tears away. "I had a turtle once, and it died. I felt real bad about, so Ma put him in a matchbox. Then Pa placed it in the corner of the garden and said a prayer. Then we sang a song and buried it."

Christopher was looking at him in a strange way.

Peter hoped that his anecdote would make Christopher feel better about losing his parents. Then he didn't quite know what to say, so he stood up, put his hands in his pocket, and shuffled his feet around. That's the same thing he did when he came out of church and Ma talked to the priest. It was a way of dealing with his awkward feelings.

Peter looked at the sad little boy on the step, and he wanted to put his arm around him and protect him. He'd never felt like that before, at least with another boy. Once, his Ma took him to another neighbor's house, and her little baby was crying. He'd tried to quiet her by holding her in his arms, but she just cried louder. So he moved away from her and pretended to be doing something else. Then her mother came into the drawing room, picked her up, and took her into the kitchen, where his Ma and the ladies were all having tea.

But that was different than what he was feeling right now. There was something special about this boy. He felt it somewhere deep down inside him. Moving closer to Christopher, he took the hankie out of his hand, stooped down, cupped his soft chin in one hand, and wiped his tears away with the other. That's what his mother always did to him, but he felt awkward trying to be gentle with him.

"Thank you." Christopher looked at him with big brown eyes that were wet with tears, then smiled.

Wow! What a beautiful smile, Peter thought. He'd never experienced anything like what he was feeling at that moment. It was kind of like a million butterflies floating in his stomach. Once, when he had a recital, his tummy was all upside down.

He'd run offstage and gotten sick in the bathroom.

But these butterflies weren't quite the same. They didn't make him feel sick; they made him feel confused. All he could think was that this boy sitting on the step beside him had red, puffy eyes. Christopher just looked at him with those big, beautiful brown eyes. It was like a huge hand reached into his heart and squeezed it so hard that he couldn't breathe. *Nope, he's special for sure.* Peter knew it; he just knew it. He was going to protect Christopher for his whole life. No one had ever made him feel this way before. *Wow, love isn't that bad after all.*

Christopher was a very open, honest person; he loved everyone. Christopher was the best thing that he'd encountered in his whole life. They quickly became best friends, exploring and discovering life together. Peter protected Christopher from all the gossip and lies that everyone had spread about him in the neighborhood. And he beat up the kids that teased Christopher and called him names.

One time, this big kid named Bud was picking on Christopher when he came out of his house. Christopher was crying because the kid was chanting "faggot" over and over again. And Christopher was yelling at him to stop, but he didn't. He just did it more. Christopher put his hands over his ears to quiet the sound, but Bud still didn't stop.

Something inside Peter snapped, and he ran over to Bud and punched him in the nose, making it bleed. He didn't stop to think about how big the kid was. All he knew was that Christopher was hurting.

Afterward, Christopher pulled Peter behind a fence in the schoolyard. There, they held hands for the first time. He remembered it like it was yesterday — the texture of his skin, the way he looked up at him. He felt like he'd just won first prize in a boxing match.

Christopher was so proud of him that he shyly kissed him on the cheek, and thanked him for being so brave. He even called Peter his hero. He couldn't get over being called that. For weeks, he never washed that side of his face.

Peter remembered the way he felt the hot blush creep up his neck and onto his face. He remembered the warmth of Christopher's lips as he touched his cheek. Yes, he remembered all of it like it was yesterday. After that day, the kids in the neighborhood never teased Christopher again. As a matter of fact, they started letting him play with them.

The two boys become inseparable. The neighborhood knew that if they saw one of them, the other wouldn't be far behind.

Soon, the boys heard whispers that some people suspected what was going on. But no one had actually seen them do anything romantic, so it was just speculation.

Somehow, the possibility of their love being forbidden made them even more passionate.

Peter loved the feeling he had when he put his arm around Christopher after he cried. He wanted him to know that he'd never leave him, even though his parents had. And he'd meant every word he'd promised Christopher. He honestly did.

Even with the suspicion, they were wonderful years.

In his prayers at night, Peter gave thanks that Christopher had been sent to him. He was secretly glad that Christopher's parents were in that accident and that he'd come to live with Mrs. Swede. Yep, he was going to ask him to marry him the day Christopher turned eighteen.

Of course, he never told Christopher that. In fact, he never told anyone that. It was his secret. He'd heard about men marrying each other in Manhattan, and he wanted to be like them. He couldn't wait for them to grow up.

***

As he reclined on the lush green grass, he allowed himself to doze off again. He'd received his weekly letter from his father, telling him about his sisters, their boyfriends, his Ma, and little Catherine. He loved to get letters from his father. They were very close and loved each other in a special way that fathers and sons do.

He opened his eyes up and looked at the sun as it sent its warm rays down to rejuvenate his worn-out body. Closing his eyes, he drifted back into his memories.

***

"How lucky I am to have met you," Peter murmured softly into his Christopher's ear.

Christopher rested in his arms at the river's edge. The sun was beating down on them, and he was happy. Every moment they shared made Peter happy; he loved Christopher with all his heart. Graduation was just around the corner, and things were changing in their lives. He would be starting a job and night school. Christopher was still in high school for one more year, and had a part-time job working after school.

They were saving their money. They'd never actually talked about spending the rest of their lives together, but Peter just assumed they would, since they'd been in love since the first day they met.

Peter wanted to make a difference as an English teacher and give children a better chance at succeeding, and Christopher wanted to be a nurse. They both had dreams and wanted to help people. Everything was good in their lives.

Then suddenly, the serenity of their moment was destroyed. They heard rustling nearby and immediately unwove their embrace, but it was too late.

Bud was staring at them.

Chapter 11
THE UNSWEET

Despite the fact that Peter had punched him in the nose when they were younger, Bud was surprisingly tight-lipped about what he'd seen. He told one person: his mother. Unfortunately for Peter and Christopher, she was very conservative and very religious, and she was friends with Mrs. Swede. And when Bud's mom learned about what her "precious angel" had seen, she was furious and marched Bud right over to Mrs. Swede's house.

Tragically, Bud's news was just the nudge that Mrs. Swede needed to take her in a direction that would not be pleasant for Peter and Christopher.

After her sister died, Mrs. Swede had started drinking every night to numb the pain. Then she started drinking during the day. She was good at hiding it from the outside world, but her friends all knew what was happening and felt sorry for her. When Christopher had come to live with her, she really hadn't wanted him, but she didn't have a choice. So any little thing would set her off, and Christopher would be the focal point of her temper.

When Mrs. Swede went on a rampage, she would take her leather belt and beat Christopher, which became a regular ritual in their house.

Soon, Peter saw Christopher's welts and bruises and wanted to help him. So he learned the rhythm of her drinking and would time surprise visits to their house. He would tell Christopher to run and hide, and he would come find him. Then Peter bore the brunt of Mrs. Swede's rage.

It didn't take long for Peter's parents to investigate the injuries he'd received. They called social services, who gave Mrs. Swede an ultimatum.

Even though she still didn't want to take care of Christopher, she used this visit as a wakeup call and started going to AA meetings. While she never fully accepted Peter and Christopher's relationship, Mrs. Swede eventually lived up to her name again.

CHAPTER 12
THE REALITY OF WAR

"Where are you?"

"I'm here, Christopher," he answered, still half asleep.

"I need you right now."

Sarge opened his eyes and looked around for the Southern voice calling him.

"Where are you? Hurry!"

The bushes behind him were rattling. He reached for the gun at his side, stood up quickly, and faced the direction of the voice. Not knowing what to expect, his heart raced in anticipation.

"Sarge?" The urgent voice was coming from the woods.

Suddenly, he realized that his time by the stream had been cut short. He stood alert, then realized it was one of his men calling to him. "I'm over here."

"Sarge! You gotta come quickly."

It was Browning, the young Southerner from his unit. He was gasping for breath and trying to talk at the same time. Relaxing his hand on the trigger, he lowered his gun to his side.

"Slow down, Browning. What's happening?"

Thoughts of Christopher would have to wait. Now he was

85

once again the efficient sergeant.

"There's been a terrible accident." Browning's face was pale and clammy.

He took Browning's gun from him and sat him down. "Put your head between your knees and breathe deep." His voice was firm as he dictated the orders to the young boy.

Browning obeyed, then lifted his head back up to look at his sergeant. Clutching his stomach, Browning stood up abruptly, darted over to the tree, and threw up. Standing by anxiously, Sarge waited patiently for him to recuperate.

"You okay now, soldier?" he inquired.

"Sorry about that, Sarge."

This young boy from Alabama had worked his way into Sarge's heart since the first day he'd arrived in his unit. He was the same age as the kid who'd committed suicide. Shaking the thought out of his head, he knew he had to concentrate on Browning.

"It's okay, kid. Happens to the best of us at one time or another. Now tell me what's going on." Sarge started pushing through the brambles, leading Browning along the overgrown path to the camp. His pace quickened as he started relaying the story.

"It happened in the schoolyard."

Sarge stopped and turned to look at Browning, hoping that he'd heard wrong.

"How many hurt?"

"Lots of them. Kids." Browning was shaking again. "Yeah, lots of kids. Little ones." His voice was weak. "Real little ones."

"Okay, calm down and tell me. Walk fast, but tell me." He calculated that it'd take ten minutes to get back to camp. "Gotta act fast."

"Bomb." Browning's voice was shallow and out of breath.

"We didn't know it was there."

Sarge stopped dead in his tracks. Browning stopped a few paces behind him. He didn't turn and look at him. He didn't want Browning to see the sick look on his face. After all, he was supposed to be the big strong sergeant, wasn't he?

Please God, don't let it be bad, he prayed to himself. Then he abruptly asked, "How many?"

Browning didn't answer. Sarge finally turned to look at Browning, "I asked you how many!"

"A dozen, maybe two. Don't know. Lots killed instantly. Maybe ten more seriously hurt. Limbs and blood everywhere. Kids screaming. Mothers and fathers trying to find their kids in the mess. Real panic. They waited to set it off until it was time to pick them up from school, so there'd be more people there."

"Damn." Sarge started running back to camp, pushing his way through the undergrowth of foliage.

"Bloody mess, sir. I came as fast as I could. I figured you'd be here by the river somewhere. You usually are."

He didn't think anyone knew that he went there to escape the horrors of war. It was his secret place.

"Are the others on alert?"

Browning didn't seem to hear him; he was racing to keep up with him. "I came here to get you as soon as I could."

"You did the right thing. Were you there? Did you see it?"

"Yeah, I was just finishing rounds, and I was passing the school in the Jeep when the bomb went off."

His voice was shaking again. He could hardly talk.

Poor kid, he thought to himself. *He won't forget this one in a hurry.*

"Keep going, soldier. We can't waste a minute."

Sarge remained calm. He'd learned to conceal his emotions. His voice was strong when he spoke. His face was lacking expression. But inside, he felt sick, thinking of the children. Sick, thinking of the parents. Damn this whole war to hell. He was just plain-old sick of it all.

What am I doing? This tour was almost over, so he knew he needed to make a decision about where his life was going. Should he sign up for another tour? Could he deal with all of this horror again?

He didn't want go home because he didn't want to face his demons or deal with reality. While he was in the army, he didn't have to think about what happened prior to enlisting—or what could happen in the future. But the stranger had unlocked Pandora's Box and made him feel again.

However, for right now, he needed to be a soldier without a heart.

"Browning, get the Jeep. Call the men out. Alert the bomb squad. I'll get the med supplies. Meet me there. Make it fast. There's no time to lose. Ten minutes, got it? TEN MINUTES!"

"Thompson is already waiting for us in the Jeep by the medical center. He sent Smith to alert the bomb squad, and I left some of the men at the school. I don't know if there're any more bombs in the yard or not. But I ordered them to rope it off, just in case."

Sarge was impressed with how efficient Browning had become. *Big change since that first day.*

"Good. Get the rest of the men ready. I'll let command know what's happening and meet you in front—"

"Already got the meds, sir. Knew we'd need them. It's all ready for us. Just need our orders."

Sarge stopped for a moment. "Browning?"

"Yes sir?"

"You did good, kid."

"Thank you, sir."

"Now head out. I'll meet you in ten. Gotta grab my stuff." Sarge needed a moment to himself, just to pull himself together. He thought of Catherine playing in a schoolyard back home. He winced.

Just then, pushing faster through the bushes, Sarge saw the camp in the distance. When they hit the opening, he ran faster and veered off towards his hut. He flung open his front door and ran inside. He grabbed several rounds of ammunition for his gun, pushed them into his backpack, and headed to the Jeep that was waiting for him. Rounding the corner, he stopped and leaned against the side of the wooden hut.

He was sweating so hard that his eyes were burning. It was yet another moment that he was grateful for the habit of carrying a handkerchief.

He lifted his head up to feel the warmth of the sunshine and closed his eyes. *Dear God, make me strong for my men.* Thoughts of Catherine entered his mind again. He took a deep breath as he straightened up. *And make me strong for Catherine.*

He opened his eyes, took a deep breath, picked up his backpack, and headed for the Jeep.

CHAPTER 13
THE AFTERMATH

Are you there?

My heart skipped a beat as I saw the soldier's message on my computer screen. It had jumped out and caught me unawares. How many weeks had gone by without a word from him?

I had finally convinced myself that our meeting was to be nothing more than two ships passing in the night. And yet, there he was on my computer screen.

I quickly wiped my hands on my skirt. *Dinner can wait*, I thought to myself. Sitting down at the computer, I pulled my chair closer to the desk and began to type. I didn't want to lose him.

Yes, I'm here.

I wanted him to know that I'd been worried about him — and to vent all the crazy thoughts that had gone through my mind.

I now firmly believed he was who he said he was, and as such, I knew the position he'd given me in his life was powerful. I had the ability to reach out to him and help ease his turmoil, or I could destroy him with one wrong word. This kind of power must be used wisely. He was young and needed someone to console him and help him through this dark period of his life. He had reached his hand out, and I was there to catch him.

How have you been?

I waited. The lapse was long. I wondered if he'd changed his mind about talking to me. So there I sat, holding my breath. Finally....

I'm okay.

Groping for words to keep him talking, I blurted out what came into my head.

I'm glad. So what time is it there? Have you eaten today?

I shook my head and scolded myself—typical mother with such frivolous questions. I'd made that mistake with my own children, and I wouldn't let it become a pattern with him.
Again, the pause seemed too long.

It's late. Another pause. *I can't sleep.*

I smiled to myself. *He can't sleep, so he's come to find me.*

Why not?

I scanned my mind for a topic that would interest him.

Thought I might catch you online.

I was thrilled. I knew I was meant to be there for him, and my doubts finally lifted from my shoulders.

What would you like to talk about?

Do you know what it's like being a soldier?

As usual, his question surprised me. I stopped to think for a moment. I tried to put myself in his place—the responsibilities, the emotions. Being responsible for young men you just met a few months ago, having to make the right decision at the right time.

No, I don't. Tell me what it's like.

You have to be tough. Do you know what it is like with all this destruction around you, night and day?

No, but I'm a good listener.

Not what I signed up for. Not at all what I thought being a soldier was.

I imagined him all alone in his little hut, missing his family and friends. The words on the screen brought me back to reality.

Pretty stupid, huh?

No, not at all. Sometimes things turn out differently than we thought they would. How were you to know?

Yeah. So many people being blown up here. Children. Body parts everywhere. Executions....

His words seem to trail off. It was as if he was sitting right there beside me. I was aware of his every move, every facial expression. It was so real, yet we were miles apart. I felt his sorrow, his fear, his loneliness.

Bomb went off in the school yard today. Not a pretty sight.

My stomach lurched. I'd never thought of little, innocent children being killed.

Were there many hurt?

I wasn't sure if I wanted to know the answer.

Yeah, too many. Too much blood.

If he'd been in the same room with me, I would've taken his hand in mine and told him how it wasn't his fault; he couldn't hold himself personally responsible. But he wasn't here, and I wasn't there. So we sat in silence, both knowing what the other was thinking. It was strange how strongly the bond between us had developed.

I won't be online for a couple of days. Something is brewing here. I'm not allowed to talk about it.

I was getting used to his manner of communicating, learning how he dealt with his issues in order to survive. Since he was solemn and depressed, I wanted to reassure him that I wanted to talk to him.

Are you going now?

Have to go to bed. Have to run five miles in the morning. I always do that, you know.

I could see his sad but truthful smile. The reality of being a soldier was sitting heavily on his heart.

This tough soldier has to stay in shape.

I laughed to myself as I envisioned myself running five miles at five in the morning, then immediately dismissed the thought. What a sight that would be.

Okay, my Stone Soldier, please find me when you can get back online. I want you to know that I'm here if you need to talk. I'm sorry about the children. I wish I could do something to take the hurt away.

My words weren't coming out very well at that moment. My mind couldn't think of anything but the children that had been killed.

Are you sure you're okay?

Thanks for the emails and the stories. They were real pretty.

I was pleased that he liked what I'd sent him. He was trying to focus on happy things. I knew that he didn't want to think of the children, and neither did I. All I knew was that he needed to be with someone tonight, and he'd chosen me.

You're welcome. I'm glad I could share them with you.

Yeah.

And just like that, he was gone.

I turned off the computer, pushed my chair out, and stood up. A smile formed on my lips. Maybe I'd made a small difference in his life. I'd been worried that I'd hurt him by allowing him to be sensitive and feeling emotions. Being a soldier was a hard job.

In my opinion, his enlistment papers should've read:

Soldiers Wanted
Qualifications:
Willing to kill.
Willing to die.
No heart necessary.
Leave emotions at home.

I would have to be very cautious when I talked with him. I didn't want to throw him off-guard.

It was dinnertime, and I was running behind. Opening the fridge, I reached in for the lettuce and tomatoes. I smiled as I realized I'd nicknamed him The Stone Soldier. After all, I didn't know his real name, and I knew it was something I'd never have the privilege of learning. So I'd have to be satisfied with calling him that.

At that moment, something inside me tugged at my heart. We would never know each other's names, never share a cup of coffee, never experience feeding ducks at the pond together. But I knew him better than I knew myself—better than he knew himself. In the short time I'd talked to him, I'd come to love him as the son I had never had. I loved him deeply and sincerely. He trusted me.

I felt inadequate. All I could offer him was an umbrella of hope and the knowledge I'd obtained during my life journey. I wasn't sure if it was what he needed, or if it would be enough. But it was all I had at that moment.

By the time the salad was made, I'd convinced myself that I was good for him. And I'd continue our conversation as long as he needed me to. I started to sing quietly as I busied myself preparing supper, and my head once again filled with thoughts of the people of Kosovo—especially the hardships of the old woman and the tragedy of the children.

Chapter 14
THE ATTEMPT

He sat at the far end of his old wooden hut. Masked in the solitude of his thoughts, the ultimate fear of identity paralyzed him. Time had become his enemy.

An eerie hush blanketed the world as night slowly devoured the day. The earth slumbered, and silence was heard. Panic evolved as the feeling of suffocation took over. Grabbing his kit and towel, he escaped into the blackness of the night. Falling into the hands of the darkness, he was left to grope along the trail to loneliness.

Rounding the corner of his wooden hut, his body keeled over. He was immersed in weakness, but he only paused for a moment to catch his breath. Sweat poured off his pale, unshaven face. Once again he tried to stand up, but the weakness was too much. Exerting every remaining ounce of his strength, he slowly stood and continued toward the shower hut, feeling his way along the darkened path.

The splinters from the old, wooden railing pierced his hands as he gripped it tightly, supporting his heavily laden body. He stumbled along, trying to stand under his own strength. The ground was covered in the innocence of frost, which filled his lungs with icy breaths of fear. He shivered in the crisp dampness as he became immersed in the feelings of inner conflict and regret.

Swallowing hard to clear his throat, he was suffocated by the black void of the future. Clutching his kit tightly to him, he entered the shower hut. Stripping his body of his blood-soaked clothing, he stood naked and vulnerable. Mechanically he stepped into the shower. His body was submerged under the full force of the hot water.

He reached for the bar of soap and started to scrub brutally, wanting to wash off the overbearing evidence of his day. Water ran down his tight, muscled body, rippling with tension as it scalded him. Lifting his head under the steam, he tried to cleanse the fear that stained his flesh. He swallowed hard to keep the emotions in tow. He felt discouraged, disheartened, and empty.

Vigorously scrubbing at the blood on his hands and arms, he tried to block out the anguished cries of the mothers. Eventually his skin became raw and bled. He weakly collapsed against the shower stall, dropping the soap to the ground.

The room's shadows became ominous as anger gave way to tears. He lifted his hand to explore the unaccustomed warmth on his taut face. Embarrassment overwhelmed him with the confirmation that the tears were his. His body shook with the images that clasped his vision, sending chills ricocheting down his chest and body.

Exhausted, he collapsed into a ball in the corner of the shower stall, rocking back and forth, his knees pressed tightly to his chest. Water continued to pelt down on him, leaving a blistering, burning sensation.

He shut his eyes, and his breathing returned to normal — hard and fast. The river of scarlet blood slowly disappeared. Tightening his throat, he felt unknown fingers press deeply into the skin of his neck, cutting off his air supply. Ghosts of the dead danced violently in the darkness of the room. Pictures flashed before him, all adding to a total admission of helplessness. With his hands pressed hard against the temples of his pounding head, he screamed, but nothing escaped his lips.

He felt ashamed of his lack of strength. Biting his teeth into his lower lip, he tried to shake himself out of these dark emotions. He thought about the young soldier he'd found dead in the shower. Now he fully understood.

He heard moaning, and he gagged as he recognized his own voice. He pounded his head violently against the shower wall, wanting the noise to stop.

Reaching for his razor, with an unsteady hand he lowered it onto his wrist. He held it carefully as he pressed it meticulously against his skin, applying pressure until the skin was slightly pierced. He watches the redness of the blood as it blended with the hot, steamy water. He sagged forward, dropping to his knees. Silence took over.

His breathing was thin as eternity took hold. A sour taste appeared in the dryness of his mouth, and his eyes opened. Shifting, he reached for his towel, wrapped it tightly around his wrist, and soaked up the bright red fluid. Gasping for air, he tried to sit up, but was tired beyond the limits of comprehension.

Shame washed over him as he became aware of how close he was to ending everything. Now he was crouched in the corner of the shower stall, rocking back and forth and pressing his knees tightly to his chest. Once again the violence poisoned his mind as he stood naked in the silence of his heavenly judge.

But the next instant, the fear subsided. An arbitrary movement determined right from wrong, and life once again prevailed.

Crawling out of the shower, he held onto the sink to help hoist himself up. Drying his face on the towel, he turned his attention to hiding his shame. Washing the blood from the shower, he wrapped his wrist in a clean bandage and covered it with his shirt. He threw his bloodied clothes into the trashcan, and buried them in the garbage.

Oblivious to everything around him, he mechanically dressed. Casually glancing into the mirror, he saw a stranger's reflection. The only remaining evidence of what had occurred was the weakness exposed in his eyes.

Two soldiers walked into the shower hut, laughing loudly to each other. He wiped his face and stuffed his razor into his kit, then zipped it closed and walked out. The soldiers respectfully saluted his rank as he passed. Sheepishly, he lowered his eyes to focus on the bare planks of wood that covered the hut's floor.

He stepped outside into the frosty night, rushed back to the safety of his hut, climbed under his rough wool blanket, and pulled it tightly around him. Thoughts of Christopher and Catherine seeped into his mind.

His body was too tired to fight the excruciating pain. He limply reclined in the claws of darkness and dissolution. Tears no longer fell. The pain had subsided, and his body slept.

Outside, the moon showered Kosovo with its golden beauty. A dog could be heard barking in the distance, and a slight breeze whispered through the trees. The night had been untouched; life went on without interruption.

CHAPTER 15
THE ROLE REVERSAL

Hi.

My soldier was back online.

Hi.

I wondered briefly where our conversation would lead us tonight.

I tried to talk to you last night, but my computer wouldn't let me. It kept knocking me off.

He was hoping I wouldn't see through his lie.

I need to talk with you. Things are happening here. I'm so down today.

I asked him what'd made him so depressed.

I'm lonely...blue...sad—

I interrupted.

Why?

The immunity of being a stranger made it safe to express our innermost thoughts, knowing that the chances of us ever meeting were a million in one.

I'm so tired.... He trailed off. *I've been taken away from my Serbs.*

This statement hit me hard. My mind raced. How was he going to handle this change? The only thing good that he'd experienced in Kosovo had been taken away from him. He loved the Serbs as if they were his family.

You're too close to them, aren't you?

I'm supposed to be this tough soldier, you know? The Stone Soldier.

He was being sarcastic. I imagined him cynically laughing.

My C.O. talked with me. He assigned me and my troop to another area, away from my Serbs.

I could feel the hurt in his words.

What'll happen to them?

Too late, I realized that was the wrong thing to write to him.

I'm not allowed to see them.

My heart broke for him. I'd come to love his compassion for them. As if reading my mind, he declared,

No, it's not my job! I'm a soldier, not a humanitarian.

I could feel the anger and hurt flowing through him.

You got too close, didn't you?

I wanted him to write the words, so he could accept the reason for his removal.

As he normally did during our conversations, he meandered for a moment. I utilized the break to compose myself.

Are you angry?

I wanted him to talk about his feelings, so he'd vent.

A little.

A lot, I retorted.

Yeah, I guess so…. But my C.O. is right. I'm a soldier.

We allowed our minds to digest that fact. I imagined the training a soldier endures. Do they train them not to have hearts and souls? I needed to back off a little to remove myself from my emotions, yet be there for him.

He's worried about me.

My soldier seemed to mellow at that thought.

He wants me to take leave. Go home for a bit.

He seemed very down about that statement.

"He's afraid I'm going to come out of this scared."

It was as if it was the ultimate embarrassment for a solider to be afraid. But isn't it human nature to be vulnerable?

Are you? Scared, I mean?

Yeah, maybe.

The tone of his words implied that he felt like a failure.

I'll just be a soldier. We're trained to be tough, remember?

He was building the bricks back up around his heart.

It's not my problem.

Nice words.

Without hesitation, I'd thrown his comment back at him.

Huh?

My words had stopped him in his tracks, made him think for a moment.

Those are just words, not your heart speaking. The Stone Soldier!

I was angry that this man was not allowed to have a heart.

So how are you?

Good change of subject.

I laughed at his tactic.

Can't talk about it, okay?

Okay, I agreed.

In fact, I wanted for him to realize that we maintained a very deep respect for each other's boundaries.

Hurts.

It's okay. Let's change the subject.

Being with you is nice.

I smiled at his comment. My role was the unknown stranger, mother, adviser, listener. The one who knew his innermost fears, deepest loves, and future dreams. That's all I could offer him, nothing more.

I'm sitting here smiling.

I imagined a 190-pound man, solid muscle, sitting at his desk with a little-boy grin on his face. And I had this power over him.

I'm glad.

I meant those words more sincerely than I'd ever meant any others.

The big bad sergeant, sitting here with a huge grin on his face. I hope no one comes in.

Are you not allowed to be happy? To smile?

Yeah, sure. But I have an image to uphold. You should know that by now. There's stuff going on over here. Can't talk about it.

He was drifting again.

How do you feel about it?

Okay, I guess. It's my job.

It sounded like he'd been given a lecture — brought back to the reality of his training.

They have no heat.

This statement seemed like it fell out of the clear-blue sky.

Who?

The Serbs. They have no heat or electricity, and it's cold.

Thoughts scrambled through my head. *Who cares if they're Serbs or Albanians? They're all caught up in the torment of war. It's cold, and they're human beings – young and old.*

Are you still there? my Stone Soldier asked me.

Yes. Sorry, I was lost in thought.

What were you thinking about?

Do you really want to know?

I didn't want to upset him, but I decided to be straightforward with him. He'd always been honest with me, hadn't he?

About the old woman you told me about.

There, I'd said it.

What about her?

I keep seeing her face in my dreams. She's so…real.

Tears welled up in my eyes, but I fought them back. He didn't answer for a moment, so I thought, *Perhaps I shouldn't have told him.*

His reply surprised me.

God! It makes the hair on the back of my neck stand on edge.

I keep hearing her words. I can't get them out of my head.

Is this too much for you?

How sweet of him. Emotionally and physically, he was a mess, yet he was worried about me. It made me admire him more.

No, it's good to realize what we have, and how selfish we can become. It's good to be thankful.

I doubt that you could be selfish.

I'd never thought of him as being kind and sensitive before.

We all are, if you think about it.

He abruptly changed the mood.

I had a dream about her too.

Tell me about it.

It was terrible.

What happened?

I dreamt that a man came to me in my sleep. I couldn't see him clearly, but he looked like Christopher.

Who's Christopher?

Then he turned into the old woman.

My curiosity was piqued, but he obviously didn't want to talk about Christopher. I'd have to wait until he decided to share that part of his life with me.

How did you feel?

I woke up in a sweat.

I replied,

I keep seeing the old woman's hollow face. Her empty eyes. The helplessness in her words. They keep replaying over and over in my mind.

It's strange how she could have such an impact on me, even though I'd never seen her face or heard her voice. His life wasn't mine, but I was living vicariously through him.

Perhaps I shouldn't tell you these things.

I'm a big girl. I can stop talking to you any time I want to, okay?

I wanted to help the only way I knew how — to reassure him that it was all right to share with me. I didn't want him to bottle up all of his feelings.

I had that dream about a week ago, and it keeps coming back to me.

I needed to tell him how I felt.

The old woman is wrong.

Why?

Because you CAN resist, and you CAN stand strong against the wind.

They were strong words, and I realized how much I believed every one of them.

Just the night before I'd dreamt of the old woman. I'd looked deep into the dark void of her eyes and seen the hopelessness of her soul. I'd told her that a bird *can* fly against the wind. That one bird can make a difference. That one bird can relay this message to another bird, and they can fly together against the wind. And many birds flying against the wind can change the world. Then suffering and illness would cease.

But if you give up hope and don't fly against the wind, then you're lost forever — waiting for death to free you.

You aren't here! You don't see what they see. What I see.

He was right. I wasn't in the middle of despair and destitution. I didn't return to my home to find it destroyed, my family dead. No job, no food to give my family, no way to keep them warm. I only had the thoughts and feelings that he'd relayed to me online. It was what he'd felt with his own heart and seen with his eyes, not mine.

Gotta go. Getting late.

Can't you talk a bit more?

I didn't want to leave things the way they were.

Nope, too much tonight.

I had to respect his boundaries.

Okay. If you'll find me again, I'll give you another story.

Yeah, I like your stories. Sorry about the mood.

You're allowed. Sweet dreams, my soldier.

You too, lady.

Over and out.

Chapter 16
THE DISTRIBUTION

Even though his Serbs had been taken away from him, he couldn't leave them. Against all orders, he continued to protect them in his small way.

The temperature dropped that night. The Serbs had to continuously burn fires to keep themselves from freezing to death. As the wrath of winter crept onto Kosovo's doorstep, things were getting scarce. The Serbs only ventured outside when necessary.

As he entered the room, feelings and thoughts raced through his mind. There were so many of them, yet he'd gotten to know them all. He could hear the silent shuffles and moans of the men and women as they moved around, trying to stay warm and comfortable. War had left its footprint—a reminder of the hell that'd taken place.

The room was a burnt-out shell of what was once an elegant, ornate home. Where large pillars once towered over smooth, white plaster, blackened timbers now stood. Scattered around the room, red and gold chairs were broken and stained with soot. The brickwork had been weakened by fire, and parts of the stairwell hung unsupported.

It was a makeshift repair to keep the bitter wind out. The walls had been repaired with branches from nearby trees and broken wood from other bombed homes. The frail roof was covered with rusty pieces of tin, cardboard, and wood. The marble tiles that had once covered the floors were now shattered and distorted. The walls were roughly patched with any materials that the Serbs could scrounge up. He could hear the wind as it whistled through the gaps in the unplugged holes.

The smell of dampness and death saturated every inch of this enormous room. In the middle, a small fire pit had been built out of debris, and everyone was huddled around it. Through the dim glow, he could see people sharing turnips that'd been cooked on the coals, and nibbling on the remains of stale bread.

The nights were getting harder to survive. The harsh winter had engulfed both the young and old. Death stood waiting. It was hard to believe that only months ago, these citizens of Kosovo were in the warmth of their homes. Now, their loved ones were dead in unmarked graves, with only the frost to keep them company.

The Stone Soldier silently made his way over to the old woman. She knew him well. Too many nights she had come to him in his dreams. Too many days he'd seen her face among the beggars pleading along the road.

This routine was now a ritual. These survivors had become his family. He'd known some of these Serbs since he'd first been stationed here.

Some of them didn't want to be evacuated because they didn't want to leave Kosovo; it was their home. Others had been separated from their family members and stayed there in hopes that they would be able to reconnect with them.

Still others had disappeared or died, and new ones had taken their place. But the old woman seemed to have an important role in the outcome of the soldier's life. She represented the pain and suffering of the war.

The soldier reached into his backpack and pulled out a small, brown-paper package. Extending his hand, he offered the package to her. Their hands touched slightly, and a shock of emotion raced through him. He pulled away quickly and stepped back into the shadows.

Opening the roughly wrapped package, the old woman carefully sorted through its contents. She took a few minutes to absorb the precious gifts that he'd given her.

Finally, she reached for the small container of fresh milk, and offered it to the child who was nestled in the warmth of her tattered skirt. The child looked up at her; his head was too large for his undernourished body, and his belly was bloated from starvation. He took the container and gulped down the smooth, rich liquid.

The old woman gently took the container from his hands and wiped his mouth. The little boy trustingly and lovingly looked up at her. Then she passed the milk to the next child. This distribution continued until the container was empty.

Hiding in a dark corner of the room, the Stone Soldier thought of Catherine's beautiful eyes and curly black hair. She looked so much like Christopher. At that moment his heart ached, realizing just how much he missed Christopher. He remembered when they'd sat at the dinner table with his parents. But most of all, in that moment, he wanted to go home.

He was tired. Far too tired. His father was right. It was time to let go of the past. A chill embraced him, and he pulled his jacket closer around him.

Just before he'd left his hut, the soldier had reached under his cot and pulled out a small metal tin. It contained a fruitcake that his mother had lovingly prepared for him. His memories of

Christmases with her were vivid, but these people needed it more than he did. He'd have other fruitcakes, but it'd be a treat for the old woman. It wasn't much, but it was the best he could do.

***

The old woman lifted the lid off the small tin and stared at the cake. Memories of happy times in her kitchen danced through her mind. Visualizing butter melting down the sides of the golden crusts of the loaves, she lined them up side-by side on the counter and allowed the happy times to creep back into her head for a moment.

The old woman tasted the fruit being prepared for a cake she'd made. She remembered that her daughter had helped her mix the batter. Her heart once again returned to the happiness they shared when they baked together.

Back in the present moment, the old woman reached into the package and found the soldier's handkerchief. She broke off a piece of the fruitcake, wrapped it carefully in the handkerchief, and placed it back in her pocket. Later, when she was alone, she'd take the cake out and remember happy times again. She handed the rest of the cake to the young girl, who quickly went about evenly distributing it among the people nearby.

***

Earlier that night, the mess hall had served steak, potatoes, green beans, carrots, and baked buns. It had been hard for the soldier to swallow the food. Every bite had lodged firmly in his throat, until he'd picked up his plate and deposited the remains of the food in the trashcan and walked away.

During his patrol he'd thought about the Serbs, and about the length of time they had to stand in line for a piece of stale bread. In these endless queues the weak often fainted and lapsed into comas, caused by starvation. The stronger ones carried on for another three or four hours, only to find that the rations had run out by the time they reached the window.

The soldier thought about the Serbian children without shoes. It was too obvious that they'd dragged small, paper-thin pieces of quilts, blankets, curtains, and quilts from under the rubble and wrapped them around their feet and hands to protect them from the frost.

That's when the idea had occurred to him. So he returned to the mess hall, retrieved the buns from the trash, and placed them in the package.

A man slipped past the soldier, which startled him back into the reality of the moment. Everyone was family. They'd taken in children who'd lost their parents, old men and women who had nowhere to go, the sick, and even the dying. The soldier watched as the old woman placed the last small piece of bun in her mouth and slowly chewed it, savoring the taste.

He thought about seeing the abundance of food on his mother's table. They were the times when he was happiest.

CHAPTER 17
THE ADDRESS

I hadn't heard from my soldier in a couple of days, and I was trying not to worry. But I had a terrible feeling in my stomach; something just wasn't right. What if he got shot? How would I know? And did I have the right to know? I didn't even know where he was posted in Kosovo. I didn't know anything about him, except his feelings.

Strange as it seemed, I'd become very close to him. I was worried about him and hoped that he would come and find me tonight. I'd been watching the news continuously, in hopes that they wouldn't report a disaster in Kosovo that would confirm my imagination. But the news was only covering other things, which were apparently more important than the aftermath in Kosovo.

I turned on my computer and sat at the kitchen table, trying to busy myself with things that needed catching-up. The big clock in the front room struck eleven; I jumped. I knew that he wouldn't be getting online tonight. It was too late for him to be talking now, so I cleared away my teacup and tidied up the table. I was just about to shut off the computer when he appeared.

I've been wanting to talk to you for days now.

I was in disbelief.

Are you there? he typed again.

I quickly typed back, trying to stop my heart from racing.

Yes, I'm here. Are you okay?

Yes. They sent me on assignment, and I couldn't get online and let you know.

I've been worried sick about you.

No lecture. He doesn't need that from you right now.

I knew you would be….

I could imagine him smiling. It pleased me that he knew I was thinking about him.

But we were forbidden to disclose any facts.

That's okay, you're here now, and you're safe.

I sighed with relief.

I finally have a few minutes on this computer, and now it's acting up. Not sure how long I can stay online before it shuts down.

He sounded tired and frustrated.

That's okay, as long as I know you're safe. That's all that matters right now. Is it cold there?

By changing the subject, I thought I could calm his mind.

Yes, it's been getting down into the thirties.

I knew he was referring to Fahrenheit, but I wasn't quite sure how it converted. I promised myself to check later.

I might get a new computer.

Why? Is yours acting up that much?

I'm pounding on the keyboard. He sounded like he was laughing. *Too hard. Must be some built-up aggression.*

He was in a great mood, light and humorous.

I got some bad news at the area meeting this morning. I have to go check on them in a minute.

I wondered what could be worse than the situation they were already in.

That's all I can say for now.

I had to respect that, so I changed the subject again.

Some of my friends and I thought we could send some mitts and scarves over to the Serbs — to keep them warm during the cold winter.

I'm sure anything would be appreciated.

Where should we send them? I know you don't parole that section anymore, but we want to make sure they get to the right people.

Send them to the commander, and he'll make sure the Serbs get them.

What's the address? How do I know which unit?

Hey, listen. I have to go. They just called for a meeting, and if I'm late, I'll get reprimanded. It's our duty to be on time. I'll let you know, okay?

I understand. No problem. When will you be online again?

I'd waited so long to hear from him, and we hadn't had a

chance to talk yet.

I'll find you when I can.

Okay, you'd better go then. Don't want you to get in trouble.

Thanks. Something big is going on here. Can't talk about it.

Sure, I understand.

I sat looking at the screen and felt empty. I wasn't sure why I had this feeling, but I did. I was getting too attached to him, and I knew it. It wasn't good. I wanted to meet him, for him to be tangible. But I wasn't sure if he felt the same way.

As I turned off the lights in the kitchen, I made a mental note to ask him for his address again. Then I could send the Serbs that warm clothing. Or was there another reason? Perhaps I just wanted another way to connect with him, so I wouldn't lose him.

Then I reminded myself that if he didn't want that, I needed to respect it.

I was just happy that he was back.

CHAPTER 18
THE EMPTINESS

Finally able to revive his ailing computer, he flipped through Merriam-Webster.com until he reached the word he was searching for: emptiness. The synonyms seemed to jump off the page that stared at him: *absentness, bareness, discontentment, hollowness.*

It's the perfect word, he thought cynically as he leaned back in his swivel chair. It perfectly fit how he was feeling. He closed his eyes, searching for any other emotion. Nothing. He just felt empty nothingness. Yes, that definitely fit the bill.

His mind ran over the last few days of his life. He'd experienced this feeling for a couple of days, and try as hard as he might, nothing seemed to jog him out of this deep, dark emptiness. He shook his head slowly, as if it would chase away the emotion. The words hung on his lips as he uttered them quietly in his mind, meticulously pronouncing each syllable. He tried to understand the word, the feeling, but there was nothing. Just an empty hole, a void of all he was—all he'd ever been.

The Stone Soldier sat still in the dimness of his office, listening to the rain tapping against the thin glass of his window. He wasn't aware of time or anything around him, except hollowness. He sat and stared at a pane as the rain heavily pelted against it, like the beating of a racing heart. A gray sadness had taken hold of him, and there was no escaping it.

Reaching into his pocket, he pulled out the harmonica his father had given him. Placing it carefully against his lips, he played a few notes of the first song he'd taught him. But the pain was too harsh. He could feel his chest swelling, ready to burst. He lowered the harmonica from his mouth.

Turning it over in his hands, he allowed himself to remember the good times. He'd had so many of them…so why did he have such a hard time recalling them? The memories he'd cherished were fading fast, and it seemed impossible to hold onto them. Nevertheless, he allowed himself to dwell in the past for a moment.

A knock at the door took him by surprise. He sat bolt upright at his desk, startled that someone had disturbed the privacy of his office.

**

"Sarge? A bunch of us guys are going to head over to the canteen to…." Stevens studied his sergeant for a moment, then continued. "We're going to see what's happening—you know, what's up. You want to come?"

Lately, Stevens had become quite aware that his commanding officer had been acting strangely. The whole troop had been talking about it.

**

He looked at the soldier standing in the shadow of the light, but he didn't hear the words he was saying. He was looking beyond the uniform to the young boy who stood in the doorway of his office. He was one of his men, yet a stranger to him.

Stevens was fair with blue eyes, was perhaps 5'6", and had a slight frame. He still had an innocence about him. *A country boy,*

119

he thought to himself. *Inexperienced with life. So young.* Would he be the next victim? Would he be the next one they'd bury? A shiver ran down his spine.

"Sarge?"

The sergeant realized that the young soldier was now standing directly in front of the desk. He quickly shuffled through some papers, trying to look busy. Looking up at the boy, he mumbled, "Sorry, my mind was somewhere else."

"So do you want to go with us?"

The Stone Soldier had a puzzled look on his face. "No thanks, Stevens, not tonight." He awkwardly smiled at the boy. Pulling open the drawer of the desk, he took out his planner. Reaching for his pen, he added, "Should get some of this paperwork finished up."

Stevens looked concerned, "You okay, Sarge?"

"Yeah." He kept his eye on his papers. "Why you asking?"

"Just that you looked kinda…." Stevens searched for the right words. "Well, I don't know, just kinda not yourself tonight."

He was alarmed at this remark. Was it that obvious? *Not good,* he thought. *Can't let my men see me like this. Supposed to be the big brave sergeant.* He shook his head as he searched for an excuse.

"Bit of a headache. Too much paperwork, I guess. Maybe I should call it a night." And with that, he pushed his chair back and stood up.

His 6'1" body looked tired. His once broad shoulders were sagging under the pressure of his emotions, and the lines under his eyes were a tell-tale sign of sleeplessness. It had been a long day; in fact, it'd been a long few months.

"Time for me to hit the sack."

"Okay, Sarge. Guess the guys and I will just go on ahead without you."

Stevens started toward the door, then stopped and turned to

face his sergeant.

"Anything I can get you, Sarge?"

"No, I'm fine. I just need a good night's sleep. If I can get rid of this headache, I'll be back to normal. You guys have a good time. Big day ahead of us tomorrow, so don't be out too late."

He didn't look up at him; he just kept fidgeting with the papers in his hands, shuffling them around like he was doing something important. Stevens bid him good night and left.

Piercing his lips tight, he took a deep breath in through his nostrils and held it for a second. His heart was racing like he'd been caught with his hand in the cookie jar.

"That was close, too close. Can't let my men catch me in a weak moment. Not good," he reprimanded himself. "Not good at all."

He was angry with himself for letting his personal emotions get in the way of his job. Each day was getting harder for him. He hated the war, what it was doing to the victims of Kosovo and to his men. He hated being away from his family. He hated the cards life had dealt him. And he especially hated the fact that Christopher was no longer there for him.

Tonight he needed him. He wanted to hear the softness of Christopher's breath as he rested in his arms. He needed to touch his long, silky hair and smell his cologne. Yes, tonight he needed Christopher more than ever. His heart lurched as a deep aching pain shot through him. Slumping down in the big wooden chair, he clutched his chest. The pain was getting worse. Closing his eyes, he breathed slowly until the pain eased off.

Reaching into the bottom right-hand drawer of his desk, he felt for the half-full bottle of Scotch. If he couldn't have Christopher, then the Scotch would have to keep him company—as it had so many nights before. Maybe the old woman wouldn't visit him tonight. Maybe, just maybe, the horrors of war would stay away.

He shoved the Scotch into his briefcase and walked towards the door. Turning off the light, he locked his office.

The rain was heavy as he ran towards the privacy of his hut. It was full-out winter now, and the air was cold and damp. He threw on the hood of his coat to keep the chill out. As he entered his hut, rain dripped off his clothes and pooled at this feet.

He didn't want to turn on the light, not just yet. Closing his eyes, he leaned his tired body against the closed door. Today seemed to weigh on him like a heavy noose around his neck. He headed across the room, threw his briefcase on his bed, reached over, and turned on the lamp. It gave off a dim, grayish light that made the shadows on the walls dance like ghosts on parade.

The rain was coming down harder and the wind had picked up, creating a howling sound that occasionally managed to creep through the cracks and into the privacy of his old hut. He threw his wet coat on the chair and reached for the bottle that was hidden inside his briefcase.

Holding it in front of him, he hesitated. Lately, drinking seemed like only thing that would keep the ghosts away. Reaching into the drawer of the nightstand, he pulled out a glass and poured the golden liquid into it until it was almost overflowing. He stared at the glass, then picked it up and pressed it to his lips. The liquid burned as it flowed down his throat.

Again, he poured the liquid and swallowed hard. This time, the burning sensation eased off. His headache was mellowing as he took the bottle and sat down on the gray army blanket that resided on top of his cot. He laughed to himself as he looked around the small confinements of his hut.

"All the comforts of home," he laughed sarcastically as he took another drink from the bottle. The hut was made of rough wooden walls. To keep the bitter-cold wind from seeping inside, there was pink insulation tucked into the cracks. On one side of the hut there was a small cot, and next to it was a table with a reading lamp on it. A gas heater sat in the middle of the room, and an army kit was placed neatly on the floor at the end of the cot. On the north side of the room was a window that looked out towards the forest area, which led to the river. In a far corner of the room was a small desk, which his laptop sat on. Army issue.

He smiled at the thought of his computer. It was his only connection to the outside world — to the stranger that he'd talked to so many times. He thought of all the stories she'd told him to take his mind off the horrors of war — the feelings of emptiness and forlornness. Once again, he chuckled to himself.

He didn't even know her name, yet he'd told her things that he'd never told anyone before. Things about the army, his feelings, his fears, and now Christopher. Placing the bottle to his lips, he swallowed long and hard. He hadn't spoken to anyone in this way since Christopher had been torn away from him. Again, he raised the bottle to his mouth, only to find it empty.

"Damn!"

Throwing the empty bottle on the floor, he stood up. He was starting to hurt again. It was bizarre how a stranger was able to see into his heart. Christopher had known him better than he knew himself. He could read his emotions, and he knew the right words to say to him. God, he loved him so much. Christopher was gone, and he was all alone in Kosovo. Isolated. He let out a long, regretful sigh.

Looking around, he realized that even his makeshift hut was better than the lodging the Serbs would have tonight. He should be grateful that he was alive.

He abruptly walked over to the computer sitting on the desk. Would she be there? Would she pull him from the darkness that'd taken hold of him? Perhaps she'd tell him another story. He loved dreaming about the stories she told. She was a good woman, and he was lucky to have found her. The soldier glanced back at the clock on the bedside table.

He opened the lid of the laptop computer and pressed start. He needed to talk tonight—to validate the emptiness he felt. He'd tell her about Christopher and Catherine. It was worth the risk. Catherine was the one thing in his life he'd avoided talking about.

Maybe it was time that he faced reality and started living again. Maybe his father was right. Just maybe.

Sitting down on the hard wooden chair, the soldier typed the online stranger a message. No response. A feeling of disappointment washed over him. He stood up and walked over to the empty bottle that was sitting on the floor. He picked it up and looked at it.

"Gotta stop drinking. It's not good for me." He flung the bottle into the trashcan by the desk, sat down at the computer, and started typing.

Hello? Are you there?

The message sat on the computer screen, unanswered.

He tried again.

Are you there tonight?

Again, there was no response to his message. He was disappointed. He needed to talk to someone. He needed to talk to *her*. She was the one person that could give him a dream that would make him forget about his past.

To him, people were people; there was no difference between Serbs and Albanians. Why couldn't this war be resolved through peaceful talks and negotiations? Day after day, village after village, the mortar shells and gunfire were heard, and the bodies piled up. Every day, everywhere he looked, there was nothing but despair.

Every day, old people wandered from building to building, searching for food to give their families. But there was always nothing. More emptiness. When would this daily humiliation end?

He hadn't felt like talking to anyone the last few days, yet he wanted to talk to her again—even with the knowledge that within five minutes, he'd be feeling emotions he didn't realize he had. She had the ability to bring them out of him.

He imagined what the stranger might say to him if she'd responded: "Are you afraid?"

"Yes, I am," he laughed to himself. "I'm afraid for the people of Kosovo. What will become of them? I'm afraid for my men, for myself. My emotions are overtaking me. It's not safe for me to be here anymore. If I can't be strong for my men, then I need to end this charade."

A buzzing noise sounded from the computer. He looked at the screen. She was online. His face lit up, and he quickly pulled the chair up to the table.

Chapter 19
The Next Day

What time?

I'd been busy working when I'd heard the IM alert.

What?

Sorry, I thought you were asking me if I was available to chat tonight. But it's already tonight there, isn't it? The time difference can get very confusing.

I hoped he was also smiling at my ambiguity.

How about now?

Apparently, he was very happy to see me. I cleared away some of the books and papers that'd been cluttering my desk.

Now is the perfect time.

I've missed you the last couple of days.

Same here. I thought you didn't need me anymore.

He sometimes had a great sense of humor, and tonight I was

reaching for it. I could sense he wasn't quite himself. I hadn't heard from him for a few days, and wondered what'd happened to put him in this mood.

Seriously?

No, no, no. I was just trying to tease you a little. I'm in a silly mood tonight.

I laughed at my lame attempt at comedy.

Been busy. I haven't had a chance to get online.

He figured a little white lie wouldn't hurt. After all, the stranger didn't know it wasn't true.

How are you feeling tonight? You seem quiet.

We have to get ready for Bill.

A change of subject was always safe. I knew the pattern. After all, we'd been talking long enough to understand each other.

My mornings are gone. But that's all right; I'll be patient for Bill.

I laughed.

Who's Bill?

The President of the United States.

Silence ensued as I tried to figure out what he meant.

Oh!

Suddenly, I felt stupid. I'd never thought about anyone referring to President Clinton on a first-name basis, and I'd never pictured him being in Kosovo. I laughed to myself.

I've been working since three in the morning, getting things sorted and ready.

Is it late there?

Yeah, real late.

I knew he was fighting his emotions tonight.

So what can I do?

I hoped it would jog the mood.

Talk to me.

What do you want to talk about tonight?

My mind was racing, trying to think of a subject.

About a very beautiful lady I contacted on here.

He'd crossed a line, which made me uncomfortable.

I guess everyone has to be patient for Bill.

I hoped to change the subject without hurting his feelings.

Are you at home now?

Yes, I have the day off today. I should be trying to cross off the things on my list, not sitting here on a computer talking to some strange soldier who's halfway across the world.

How nice for you.

I was worried. He seemed to have closed himself off to me, which wasn't good.

Yes, it is. I love my days off.

I can tell.

How?

By the way you write.

I could see him leaning back in his chair with a smug look on his face, enjoying every moment.

I'll bet you have that goofy smile on your face. I laughed out loud.

Hey, it's not that goofy.

Now I had his attention. That was good.

Okay, maybe not, but it's as goofy as I imagine it to be. After all, I don't even know what you look like. So I can picture you any way I want.

I was having fun with him, and continued.

Hmm, the visual. Or lack thereof. Does that mean I can let my imagination run wild too?

I knew he was teasing me, but I also knew that there was a fine line — and that he was lonely.

Well, I don't think you should, unless you want a scary picture of me to pop up in your mind. I'm sitting here with a goofy smile, in my battle fatigues at a small desk in my hut. Is that enough of a visual for you?

More than enough, thank you.

A picture would help though, don't you think?

No, because the truth is that you wouldn't talk to me if you saw me. I'm a huge over-the-hill woman with one brown eye and one blue eye. And of course, there's a wart on the end of my nose. And I'm sitting here filling my face with Twinkies while I talk to a soldier I've never met.

I reached for Twinkie that sat beside the computer, then hesitated. "Perhaps not," I laughed as I put it back on the plate.

Just my type, he wrote back.

By then, I was laughing so hard that tears were streaming down my face.

I bet you're laughing at that visual.

Oh yes, not a pretty picture at all!

Good, glad I could make you laugh. Although some of that is true, unfortunately.

The blue-and-brown eye part?

No! The Twinkies and…. Well, it's still not a pretty picture.

I wasn't sure what to say; it was an awkward moment. We'd both silently agreed not to exchange any personal information. Hadn't we? We'd both opened the door to our hearts and emotions and allowed each other to see our true selves. We'd filtered out the untruths, thrown away the concealed realities, and given each other the kind of trust that one wonders if they'll ever find again. Yet we still hadn't disclosed our real names.

So many times I'd envisioned his face, blurred behind the façade of a soldier. Frightened. Struggling desperately to stay within the molded expectations of society. But he'd chosen to talk to me that night we met.

So, my dearest friend, I have to hit the sack. No rest for the wicked.

Okay then, I'll let you go. Promise you'll find me in a few days?

Sure. It all starts again tomorrow.

Are you okay?

I just needed to see the words from him.

It's life, right? Sweet dreams, my friend.

He was in a strange mood tonight. Each time we'd talked, it'd been getting harder and harder to reach him. Depression was overtaking him.

Sometimes we spoke every night. And then there'd be times when I'd wonder if he'd decided not to share his life with me anymore. It was hard being the stranger on the other side of the world.

***

Staring at the lid of his laptop, he remembered that their entire conversation was being monitored by his superiors. He realized that he'd wanted to tell the stranger about Christopher, but he couldn't. Sharing his thoughts about him would've made his memory fade even farther away from him, and he couldn't afford that luxury. At least, he couldn't for now. Perhaps another day.

He shut down the computer, went over to the cot, and lay down. If he got caught talking about his feelings to the stranger too much, she might be blamed for taming the lionhearted. But he could still dream about Christopher. Closing his eyes, he allowed his beautiful memories to envelop him.

Chapter 20
The Picnic

He'd sat up in bed and realized what a special day it was going to be. It was Christopher's eighteenth birthday — a beautiful summer day. He'd waited a long time for this day.

He quickly showered, dressed, and headed down the street to Christopher's house. They were going to the river for the day, just the two of them. The time had passed too quickly, and he didn't want to leave this paradise. He longed to stay beside the river with Christopher forever.

"Hurry! We're going to be late, and then we'll be in trouble." Christopher was putting the food and dishes back into the picnic basket.

"Can't we stay a little bit longer?" Peter mumbled, lazily lying back and enjoying the sunshine. He turned onto his side to admire Christopher.

"We're not going to be late for my birthday dinner if I can help it. If we are, your mother will dart knowing looks at me, imagining all the terrible things we've been up to."

"Hmm…. Were they really that terrible?"

"Oh, you're impossible. You know my aunt. She'll sigh and

judgmentally cluck at me."

Peter reached up, pulled him down onto the blanket beside him, and started kissing him. Christopher squealed and pretended he didn't like it. But as a matter of fact, he knew he liked it a lot.

"Stop it," Christopher giggled. "This is serious."

"I am serious," Peter murmured. "In fact, I'm more serious in this moment than I have ever been in my entire life."

Christopher struggled in his arms, trying to break free. "You've never been serious since the first day I met you." Finally pulling away from his grip, he sat on the blanket and straightened his hair.

"I've been serious before. Lots of times," Peter sulked.

"Uh-huh." Christopher's nonchalant reply implied that he didn't believe him and wasn't really that interested. He had a way about him that made him feel like he always needed to explain himself. Christopher was flashing that coy smile of his, lowering his eyes from his gaze in a seductive way that made his heart race.

"Actually, I was very serious the first day I met you. I even wiped away your tears."

Sadness clouded Christopher's eyes, and his voice was quiet and low. "Okay, maybe you were that day. I'll never forget how kind you were." Christopher lifted his eyes up to meet his, trying to look firm. He added, "But you haven't been serious one day since then."

"No?" He sat up quickly, pretending to be annoyed.

"No," Christopher firmly repeated as he straightened the wrinkled material in his shirt, so his aunt wouldn't guess what they'd been doing.

"Never?"

"Never!"

Christopher's eyes twinkled with mischief as he confirmed

his question. Then he tilted his head to one side and looked at him with those beautiful brown eyes. Christopher didn't realize that when he looked at him that way, Peter wanted to give him the world.

Peter was surprised at the depth of the emotions that ran through him at that precise moment. The words he wanted to say stuck in his throat, but he swallowed hard and took his hand.

"Then always remember this moment, because I'm more serious right now than I'll ever be again."

He stood up, then got down on one knee. He again took Christopher's hand in his and deeply studied the love and tenderness in those big brown eyes. He wanted to memorize how handsome he looked at this moment. Etch it into his heart.

In that moment, Christopher was his very soul, the air he breathed. He was his one and only love. Words couldn't sufficiently describe how Christopher looked as he sat on the blanket, waiting for him to speak. His eyes filled with love for him. His sensual lips parted, inviting Peter to kiss them. At that moment, he wanted Christopher more than he'd ever wanted anything before. His feelings were so strong that he could barely control them.

Christopher sat still on the blanket, like a toy patiently waiting in a store window. He was the picture of perfection, and he knew that his heart belonged to him. He could see the love reflecting in Christopher's eyes. He could feel it, encasing and holding him. Yes, he loved him.

"Christopher," he whispered in a soft, low tone, pausing for what seemed like an eternity. The extent of his love for him was so boundless that he wept. So he buried his face in the palm of Christopher's hand, kissing it gently.

Peter was still frozen to the spot. The moment stood still as he looked deep into Christopher's eyes.

"Always remember this." Peter paused to take a breath and ease the pain of his heart pounding. He cupped his hands around Christopher's heart-shaped chin, and moved closer to him. Then he continued speaking the words he'd practiced for so many years.

"I love you." Peter's words choked on the emotion, so he started again. "I love you more than life itself."

Tears welled up in Christopher's eyes. He searched Peter's face for the sincerity of his words.

"I've loved you since the moment I set eyes on you...." Peter paused, trying to catch his breath. "I can't imagine a day passing by without you in my life."

The tears were gently falling down Christopher's sweetheart face. Emotions were running wild in their hearts. Peter took his finger and gently brushed the warm tears away, just like he had on that day so long ago.

"Don't cry, Kit. I'm here, and I'll never leave you." Again, he wiped away the tears that pooled on the dampness of his cheek. "You're the best thing that's ever happened to me. I love you. Do you hear me, Christopher? I want to marry you. I want you to be my husband."

Peter reached into his pocket and pulled out a handsome gold band. He held Christopher's hand and easily placed the ring on his slender finger. Then he raised Christopher's hand to his lips and kissed each finger, one at a time.

"I don't care what other people say. I want to stand by you forever. I want to love you more and more each day. I want to have a family with you, and grow old together. I want to sit in a rocking chair and tell you how happy you've made me over the years. I want to share the good and bad times with you.

"I want you to lie in my arms. I want to make love to you under the stars until the night makes way for the morning. I love

135

you," Peter whispered. "I love you so much...." Taking a deep breath, he continued. "I loved you the moment we met, I love you now, and I will love you forever and beyond. Marry me."

His heart pounded heavily as he tried to swallow the emotional lump that'd formed in his throat. Christopher didn't reply, and Peter started getting nervous.

Christopher was just staring at him, not saying anything.

What if he doesn't love me like I love him? he realized. Panic set in. He hadn't thought of that until now. *What a fool. What if he's not ready to do something this unconventional? Could he be embarrassed about a public ceremony?*

He had just assumed that Christopher would want to marry him.

Peter fidgeted in the silence. Christopher was in a state of shock, and he still hadn't answered. He sat very still on the blanket, frozen to the spot. His tears had stopped now. His face had turned a shallow shade of white. He was uneasy. Still so young, he'd never trusted anyone so deeply and sincerely.

What if he refuses me now? Then what? Would that be a betrayal? Is it his prerogative to not want to be so forward-thinking? Some gay people actually like being on the fringe of society. Maybe he just wants to keep it quiet.

"Christopher?" He queried nervously, scanning his face for an answer.

Christopher's lips opened, and he swallowed hard. "I...." Christopher began again. "I...." That was all that escaped his lips. He lowered his head.

Peter looked at him expectantly. Not able to stand the silence any longer, he babbled, "I mean, I always thought we would get married." *Damn*, he thought to himself. *Why can't you find the right words when you need them?* He soldiered ahead, muttering, "I just assumed you felt that way too. The first day I met you, I knew I wanted to marry you. You looked so sad and lost...."

He lifted Christopher's face towards him. Christopher started sobbing uncontrollably, and hid his face in his hands.

"Oh my God! Christopher?"

Peter took Christopher in his arms and pulled him tightly to him, rocking him back and forth.

"Please don't cry. I'm sorry. I didn't mean to make you cry."

Peter didn't know what to do. He felt sick inside. *How could I hurt Christopher like this*? he thought. *I'm a stupid fool.*

But instead, Peter whispered, "It's okay. Hush now. Don't cry."

He lovingly stroked Christopher's dark wavy hair.

"Hush, Kit," Peter cooed as he clung to him, sobbing. "It's okay if you don't want to marry me. I just thought.... Oh damn! I don't know what I was thinking."

He was at a loss. Christopher's thin body was throbbing.

"Are you okay, Christopher?"

Christopher gently pushed himself away from Peter. "I don't know."

Taking Christopher's hand in his, Peter sadly touched the ring on his finger. "Just forget I asked you to marry me, okay? It really wasn't that important. It was just kinda.... Well, sort of a—"

Christopher flung himself into his arms and held him tightly. Peter was shocked.

"Pete," Christopher whispered. "When that boy saw us...."

After Peter realized why Christopher was silent, he calmed down. Finishing Christopher's thought, he used a comforting tone. "He was shocked. And there was some talk. But I didn't see any pitchforks."

"I'm pretty sure my aunt had a torch ready to go," Christopher joked.

"A mob of one," Peter added.

They laughed.

"Christopher, I can promise you two things: I will always protect you, and I will never leave you."

Christopher pulled Peter close to him and held him very tightly. He didn't ever want to let him go. "My soldier of pride...."

Peter didn't know what to make of this proclamation.

"I didn't think you'd ever ask me," Christopher murmured.

"Is that a yes?"

"Yes," Christopher whispered, and nuzzled his face into his neck. "Yes, yes, yes."

"Christopher, my one and only love, I adore you so much." They kissed deeply and passionately.

***

He suddenly awoke to find that he was no longer by the river with Christopher. Instead, he was in his cold, dreary hut in the middle of a war-torn country, which he'd never even heard of when his true love turned eighteen. His slumbering memory had transformed into the nightmare of his reality.

He pulled himself out of bed and moved to stare out the window at the gray blackness of the sky. He couldn't shake off the gnawing feeling that clutched at him: Just like fighting an enemy, he was battling to win his life back. The days were harder now, and he was lonely. Time hadn't healed his wounds; it'd just left him standing in the perils of depression. Deep thoughts entwined themselves around his heart as his mind wandered.

What was the purpose of life without Christopher? At this point, he was at an emotional standstill—simply going through the motions. Like a marionette, he didn't know where he was going or what he was supposed to do. It seemed as if everyone else was pulling the strings and knew the script, yet he kept wandering aimlessly through the gloom of the labyrinth.

He contemplated, "I've never been in this perimeter of life before. These feelings frighten me." The rain tapped on the window pane, keeping rhythm with his heart. "How did I travel to this bleak, forbidden space? Where is the version of myself I used to know so well? Perhaps he never really existed. Sometimes I wish life could be easier, but I know it isn't. I know in my heart that I must continue walking along this dark path through the woods until I come to an opening, where the light will shine down on me once again.

"Yes, I know such a place exists, for I've been there. I've lived it. I've experienced the ultimate dream of happiness. And maybe if it's meant to be, I'll open my eyes, and that dream will be my reality."

The night was quiet with blackness. He thought, *Tonight, the people of Kosovo are at rest.* Slowly, his faith in his ability as a soldier diminished. He'd promised to fight for his country — his family, friends, and loved ones. But this war was taking its toll on him.

He laughed out loud as he mocked his fate. Reaching to turn out the light, he promised himself that tomorrow would be a better day.

But his feelings overwhelmed him as he lowered himself back onto the cot. As he buried his head in his hands, despair quietly crept through the empty walls of his room. His voice rattled with pain and anguish as he whispered, "Christopher...." His body twisted and turned with the agony he felt. In the emptiness of his hut, his heart echoed back to him, "Christopher...."

Chapter 21
THE AMBIGUITY

Hi, can you talk?

I hadn't seen my soldier online for several days, and I was worried. I couldn't wait any longer for him to contact me.

Are you there?

I wanted him to pacify the gnawing feeling that something had happened to him.

Hi.

I was relieved to see his reply.

Hold, he typed.

Okay.

Had to shut the door. Didn't want anyone to walk in and catch me on here.

He seemed to be good spirits.

How've you been? I haven't heard from you.

140

I can talk right now, but please understand that I'm not alone today. And we may be interrupted.

All right. I just wanted to make sure you were okay.

Today was busy, mostly paperwork.

Are you feeling better?

No. My C.O told me that my stance on the issue reinforced his opinion. I need to back off.

Oh. I hesitated, then added, *You know, he's just concerned about you.*

There was no reply to my remark. Impatient, my fingers fidgeted with the pen that sat beside my keyboard.

It's not good to get personal over here. He said he'd watched a sniper transform into a member of the Peace Corps. He ordered me to see a psychiatrist.

I could feel his shame as a soldier. That was a very harsh pill to swallow.

It's for your own safety.

Yes.... But it's really gotten under my skin.

I know.

And it hurts. Easy to stay away, shut things out.

You're a soldier, and he's right. As much as I hate to say it, he's right. You're supposed to remain impartial.

There're plenty of other things to do, but I keep wondering how my Serbs are doing.

141

We both sat in silence for a few minutes, wondering. We'd developed a channel of understanding without talking, and respected each other's opinions and feelings.

I stopped taking them rations and money.

You brought love and happiness to them. Even if it was only for a brief period of their lives. They knew there would be a time when it would all stop. You're a soldier, and soldiers come and go. But they loved you in return for your compassion and caring.

And what'll happen when I stop showing up? How will they buy food? The children, the sick, the old.

I imagined him sitting back, folding his arms across his chest, and heaving a sigh of frustration.

How could you understand all this?

They know you're following orders. They understand you were a gift to them. Please trust me on this; they don't think you abandoned them.

He was waiting for the anger to ease up.
I tried to reiterate my point.

They knew you couldn't stay forever. I was getting desperate.

Finally, he replied.

I have some of my men checking on them for now. Until they get caught.

You gave the Serbs all you could. You couldn't do any more for them. They understand this is war, and they'll never forget your kindness.

So where do you draw the line?

I jumped through the door he'd left open for me.

You need to back off. Those are your orders, and you're a soldier.

But he snarled, *It's doing the right thing vs. doing your job.*

He was being so cynical.

I snapped back, *No! Not at all. It's time to give them back. They need to learn to survive by themselves. I know it's unfair. Life is not always the way we want it to be. It's like letting your child fall off his bike all the time. You know you have to let go, so they can learn. But it still hurts you to watch it happen. But in the end, they succeed.*

Wow!

I stared at the word, not knowing exactly what he meant. But soon enough, he clarified himself.

I didn't expect you to understand how I was feeling, but you seem to understand it better than I do myself. Thank you! It all makes more sense now.

I could feel him smiling as I continued.

Life teaches you lessons. Life goes on, and we learn to cope. Your time with the Serbs is done now. You have to let go.

But it hurts.

It'll hurt you more than it'll hurt them. It's time.

Maybe I just wanted to take care of someone.

Is there anyone else you could take care of?

Catherine.

Are you ready to talk about her?

143

You're making me too soft for my environment.

I hope not. Or I'll have to let you go. And that would crush my heart, my friend. I hesitated for a moment. *But I've actually been mulling over the same thing, so it's finally time to address it: Am I really making you too soft?*

My heart was pounding, and my stomach was churning. I waiting for the answer I wanted to hear.

I'll stay. For now, I'll stay. He paused. *I feel blessed that you've taken the time to talk with me.*

The first night we met, your heart called out to me. I believe that people come into your life for a reason.

That's very wise.

Wisdom comes with age. And believe me, I'm aging fast. I tried to lighten the mood.

I feel like a chapter is closing.

His remark caught me off-guard. But suddenly, I knew it was true. He'd move on, and I wouldn't be part of his life anymore. He'd outgrown me. The thought made me shiver with sadness. I had come to love this stranger like one of my own children. I choked back the tears.

Perhaps it is.

Why've you been here for me?

I took my time crafting an answer.

It was meant to be.

You must've had something to teach me.

Maybe it's you that had something to teach me. Destiny is never clear.

Perhaps you needed to learn something about soldiers. Those that kill for their country still have a heart. A dedication that few can understand.

I wasn't sure how to respond to that statement. I wasn't sure about anything anymore. There was a long silence.

Are you still there?

I was thinking.

About what?

It's not that I've learned why soldiers do what they do. It's that I now understand how they feel. Will you talk to your C.O.? Tell him you've come to terms with this? He worries about you.

Hold a second.

I awaited his return.

Sorry, have to go.

The end to the conversation was abrupt. I was left wondering what'd happened. Nevertheless, I logged off and headed to bed.

But I couldn't sleep. I kept thinking about him, and about the Serbs—what they'd do now, especially now that winter was here. I was so confident about my advice to my Stone Soldier, but inside, my heart was worried about the Serbs. I knew exactly how he was feeling, but I wondered about the old woman. Would her question ever be answered?

CHAPTER 22
THE RELEASE ORDER

Have you seen any of your ducks, my beautiful friend?

I smiled when the message appeared on the screen of my computer.

Hi there, I typed.

We've been swamped.

I ventured to reply, *I missed our conversations.*

Me too. The whole place is going nuts, getting ready for the big visit.

When is it?

December 23.

Wow, that's soon. Is everything ready?

Our conversations had taken on a casual tone lately. It was like settling into a comfortable pair of slippers. It was nice.

Yes. Just got a break a few minutes ago, and I'm waiting for our

146

next meeting.

Well, I think the 190-pound soldier with the big grin on his face will impress him, don't you? If not, then show him your gun. That should do it.

I don't think he'll be impressed by that. You know, I have this good friend who calls me the Stone Soldier. Can you believe that?

Hey, I'm just teasing you a little today.

That's okay. I like it.

I knew he was laughing at the thought of us bantering like school kids. It felt good to be light-hearted.

Good, then it's just what you need, and I'm glad it helps.

Thank you for your kindness.

Just trying to be a friend.

We're scheduled to leave here on New Year's Eve.

Because the president is coming?

We were supposed to go to Greece to ship back to Germany, but the Greek port is closed.

Why are you going to Greece to ship back to Germany?

The port for shipping our equipment, weapons, and trucks is in Greece.

But Kosovo is in Eastern Europe, right? The Balkans.

Maybe they'll truck them there.

The weapons? I'm so confused right now, it's like a riddle. I laughed out loud.

Want to know where your Stone Soldier is going?

Of course.

He's headed home.

His statement changed everything. I'd never considered the fact that he'd leave Kosovo soon. I wondered if we'd continue our conversations once he got home.

This tour of duty is over, and I've decided not to do another one. Now I can go back to being human.

His words conveyed a sigh of relief. He didn't realize just how uptight he'd been all these weeks. Obviously, he was delighted that he was being shipped out. As for me, I had mixed feelings.

I can wear civilian clothes again, have days off, eat real food.

You don't eat real food?

Ever try mess hall food?

No, I haven't.

Consider yourself lucky. He paused. *I'm tired. I want to get away from it all. I want to be an English teacher.*

Do you have your teacher's degree?

No, a couple of courses short of it. Was almost there when…. I'm going to get a state certification.

What does that involve?

Take the state test and do student teaching. I already have most of my courses, so I'll challenge the board for my degree.

Sounds wonderful.

Education is always a good thing, and he'd make a great teacher.

Then I can teach in several states, he added in a dream-like state. *My guys say that they can't imagine me teaching kids.*

Why not?

Sorry, gotta go now. I'll try to find you later.

One of his soldiers must've entered his office.

Okay, I'll watch for you.

Oh, I wanted to tell you something, but it'll have to wait. It's about what happened to me before I joined up. I think it'll explain a lot. It's time I told someone.

He seemed pleased that he could finally talk about his secret. Was he going to tell me everything? Was he going to explain where Christopher was, and how Catherine came into his life? Was he really going to let me see behind that cold stone wall of his?

I went to reply, but he'd already logged off. He'd left me staring at the computer, trying to figure out what he meant. Trying to sort out all the information he'd given me.

Going home would definitely be good for him. Finally, he'd find some peace of mind, go back to school, become an English teacher, and be happy. I was smiling as I thought of all the things he wanted to do, but inside, I had butterflies in my stomach. What was this secret he was ready to tell me?

I wasn't sure where our friendship would go from here. I'd become attached to this young soldier, but I didn't know how he'd feel about continuing our friendship after he was back with his family. Would he need me in his life anymore?

Sadness enveloped me as I shut down my computer and went about my workday.

CHAPTER 23
THE HOMECOMING

The day had been long. The burden of his duties as a soldier, the excitement that he and his men were about to go home, the anticipation of the president's arrival. The end was so close.

He was going home. Home to his family. Home, where he could finally finish his degree and follow his dream. But most importantly, home to Catherine. It'd been far too long.

His father was right. Every letter he'd sent begged him to come home. Time and time again, his father told him that Catherine needed him, but she consistently reminded him about the unforgettable promise he'd made to Christopher in his darkest hour.

He knew it was finally time to try to forget the past. No, not forget, but move on, and start a new chapter.

The briefing had been long. He didn't like the orders that his C.O. had given his troop. He just had a feeling.

He grabbed his jacket and headed down the path to the river — the spot that he'd come to love. It was the one place where his thoughts felt like his own. There, he could be with Christopher again and enjoy the happy times they'd once shared.

Heading through the thick brush, he ran down the trails until he could hear the roar of the river. The crispness of the breeze felt good on his face. He found his spot near the riverbank, threw his coat on the green grass, and plopped down.

Soaking up the sun's rays, he felt rejuvenated. He'd finally stopped hibernating and wanted to live again. The winter of his life was over. This feeling was almost too much for him, so he allowed the silence of Mother Nature to wrap him in her cocoon.

The reflections of winter's rain were obvious as the river rushed wildly past him in a luscious melody. The mocking sky covered the sun with a small grey cloud, then blew the cloud away to reveal the golden warmth of its rays. The last of the autumn leaves rustled as they fell to the ground like petals from a rose. He was caught between eternity and time.

His coal-black eyes were no longer laden with sadness. Immortality unveiled its calmness, and he felt happy. For the first time in years, he felt happy. Above him, a raven was flapping its slow wings across the vastness of the open sky.

Christopher had loved the wind. He loved all nature. He wondered if Catherine also loved it so deeply and passionately. He wondered what his little girl looked like now; it had been so long.

She was so small when he'd left—just a little baby. He shivered at the memory. His mother had taken her home that terrible night, and he'd refused to see her after that.

He'd held Catherine at the gathering, but he didn't want to. He didn't want to feel her warmth in his arms. He just couldn't bear seeing her resemblance to Christopher. He couldn't stand seeing the way her trusting brown eyes stared at him, or the way the blackness of her hair framed her tiny tan face like Christopher's.

He quickly gave her back to his mother. He left town the next day and never went back. She'd be raised by his grandparents—

without her fathers.

"How could I have done that? Catherine, will you ever find it in your heart to forgive me? I promise that when I get home, I'll make it up to you. I'll be the best father anyone ever knew. I promise."

A sadness enveloped him. He wouldn't break this promise. He'd never break a promise again.

The river rapids relentlessly pounded the banks, eating away at them inch by inch, like the pain that ripped his flesh away. He thought of his promise to Christopher. How could he not have kept it? His heart was heavy. He'd broken his promise; it was his last wish. He'd make it up to him and Catherine. He was going home, and he'd finally be a father.

"Sarge?" came the familiar voice from the woods. "Sarge, you there?"

Browning rounded the path and headed towards him. After the school incident, Browning had shared this sanctuary. Sometimes bringing cookies and iced tea, they'd just sit together watching the river and feeling the energy from the sun. They'd grown very close to each other. Occasionally Browning would break the silence by reciting a poem or sharing his life's dreams. Other times they just sat in silence without needing words. He'd come to like this kid a lot, and he was sad they'd have to part soon.

"Thought I'd find you here."

Browning sat down beside him and drew his legs up to his chest.

"Pretty here, isn't it?"

"Yeah, it really is."

They quietly listened to the river gurgle and spin.

"Everything okay, Browning?"

"Yep, everything's fine. Finally."

"Yeah, me too."

They both sat staring at the river. The peace they'd found mesmerized them.

"Sarge, can I ask you something?"

Browning apprehensively shuffled his foot in the warmth of the dirt. "Sure, you know you can."

"I heard we're going into the Russian sector after the president leaves."

"It's not official yet, but there's a good chance." He tried to sound calm.

"There're rumors about it being a dangerous mission. Is that right?"

"Every time we go out it's dangerous," he replied a little too abruptly. He didn't want Browning or the others worrying. It's not good to worry about a mission; that makes it less safe.

"The guys are saying that they don't want to go. Too many rebels and snipers...." Browning lowered his head.

"We're soldiers. It's our duty to protect the innocent. We're trained for missions like this." In a softer, more compassionate voice, he added, "It'll be just fine. Besides, we haven't gotten the official orders yet, so it might not happen. Just focus on going home, okay?"

"Yes sir." His reply had an underlying tone of uncertainty.

Browning was turning out to be a good soldier. He was still young, but what he learned, he learned well. He'd taken a real liking to him that first day. He could be bitter and cocky, but he had a good heart. He'd kept him nearby, so the younger man wouldn't get shot.

"Well, I just wanted to hear the words from you, sir. Didn't want to get all stirred up over things without you backing them up." He paused. "If you know what I mean." Browning stood up and brushed off his pants. "Well, it's dinnertime. You comin',

Sarge?"

"Be there in a bit. Just want to take in the last of the day."

"It sure is a pretty place. I'll be sad to leave it—I mean, the river and all."

"Yeah, but there's a whole new life waiting for us back home. Always another door opening."

Browning smiled and recited a line from "The Road Not Taken" by Robert Frost, then turned and headed back to camp.

The river leapt as it raced downstream, over mossy boulders and through treacherous bends, until it widened out. There, the water swirled until it became calm and serene. The effect was quite exhilarating.

One could see the dark of the forest in the distance. The sun was setting in majestic wonder, imparting a golden tinge on the trees. Nature blazed on the hillside, throwing a chilling brightness over the chaotic mass of rocks and bushes. The thick green forest danced with mystery, as day elegantly disappeared into the twilight.

Sarge reached into his pocket and pulled out his picture of Christopher. It'd been a few weeks since he'd last looked at it. The pain had been unbearable, but now it'd eased. He was so handsome. He gently kissed the picture.

"I'm coming home, Christopher, and I'll finally keep my promise to you. I love you."

He put the picture gently back into his pocket and pulled out the harmonica his father had given him. He hadn't played for a long time. Wetting his lips with his tongue, he slowly raised the harmonica and placed it firmly in his mouth.

He started playing "I'll Be Loving You Always."

He felt the tears escape from beneath his eyelids. His lip began to quiver, but he kept playing. And when the song was finished, he put the harmonica back into his pocket and stood up.

Turning slowly, he bid goodbye to the river, and to all the darkness that'd encased him the last few months. He sighed deeply and headed back to camp.

CHAPTER 24
THE WAITING GAME

Did you feed the ducks today?

Silly, I don't live on Denman Island. That's where I grew up.

Oh, I didn't realize that. Hmm, that's a shame. You seem to love it there so much.

Yes, one day I'll go back.

You should. We should all do what makes us happy.

I couldn't believe his change of mood. He was finally glad about going home. But I was unsure of everything between us now — and a little sad.

So how are things going over there? I asked cautiously.

About normal. For here, that is.

Okay, I know you can't talk about it, and I respect that.

Did you work today?

No, I had the day off, so I cleaned the house and went to visit a friend. Usual stuff.

I thought to myself and laughed, "Boring stuff." But I didn't type that.

Did some paperwork and caught up on things. I'm brain-dead now.

Hmm, I can't imagine your brain being dead. You're very smart, you know.

Really? I smiled at the compliment.

Yes, you're so wise about things.

Oh, that isn't true. I've just lived longer than you.

Unfortunately, I don't have much time.

I know. You're always busy.

I was disappointed, but I didn't mean to show it. He didn't need me anymore. I felt very left out of his life, like it was all ending.

Bill is arriving tomorrow, but we won't be here.

Where are you going?

The Russian sector. Wasn't supposed to be until after Bill's visit, but it got pushed up.

My heart lurched. I knew he was waiting for my reaction. I could feel the uneasiness in his words.

Is it dangerous?

Depends.

Be careful.

I reached up and touched my lip. I'd sunken my teeth into it, causing it to bleed. The pain was sharp.

Always am.

His answers were too short. I didn't like the vibe I was getting from him. He'd never been afraid before, so I knew this mission was going to be different.

I think I have my priorities back in line.

He was trying to be to be the official soldier, but he wasn't fooling me. An aching sense of loss crept through my body.

Concentrate on what you're doing, okay?

Everyone has their lot in life.

My hands were shaking.

Don't you think you're overreacting?

It just gets a little confusing when you go from peacekeeper to killer.

Do you really think of yourself as a killer?

Especially when there's no peace to keep.

I was trying to figure out where this mindset was coming from, but I couldn't.

Even when I was a kid, I spent most of my time playing soldier on the streets of the Bronx — at least until I met Christopher. And of course we played football.

So perhaps you were meant to be a soldier?

Nawh.

There was silence on the other end, and I knew he was deep in thought. There was so much happening in his life at the moment. His head must've been spinning. I could feel the excitement about his plans for the future, but I could also feel my own curiosity. I couldn't contain myself anymore; I had to ask.

You were going to tell me something the other day, but you suddenly got called away.

Yeah, I wanted to tell you about Christopher.

So who is he?

Well, it's a long story. I have to head out in a few minutes for another briefing, but I'll find you when I get back. I'll explain everything then. I thought you deserved to know, especially after all the dreams you've shared with me. I've been waiting for the right time.

Okay. I was disappointed, but I understood. *Stay safe, okay? This old gal worries about you.*

I didn't want him to go. Inside, I had a bad feeling about it—a premonition.

Till tonight.

So much had happened and changed since we first met. It'd left me wondering just what'd happen to him next. Too many questions were unanswered. Tonight I'd learn about Christopher, and I'd ask him about our friendship.

Perhaps we'd even exchange real names. I'd thought about it for a long time, and I decided that I wanted him to know my name. I was content with my decision. I wanted to meet him one day. But for now, I'd have to wait patiently.

CHAPTER 25
THE BAD FEELING

Hi.

He was back. I'd made sure I left my computer on, just in case.

Hi. How was your briefing?

You know, if you've been to one, you've been to them all. He laughed.

That interesting, huh?

I wanted to share something with you.

There was a long silence. I wasn't sure if I should pursue the issue, or just leave it hanging.

I've never talked about Christopher before. He paused again. *Or Catherine.*

Okay.

But I can't talk about it now. I have to get up early in the morning, and I'm exhausted. Too much emotion. I'll send you an email about it tomorrow.

I understand.

I thought it'd be better to read the email before pursuing the topic.

Read the letter, okay? It'll explain a lot. And when I get back from this assignment, we can talk about it. I want to share this part of my life with you.

Thank you for trusting me.

For some reason, I felt sick inside. I didn't like the assignment he was undertaking. And I wasn't sure what the email would contain. I wanted him to reassure me that he was going to be safe, which he did.

All assignments are dangerous.

I know, but you seem —

I can't really talk about it.

I let my fingers trail over the keyboard without pressing any keys. My mind was racing like someone had just thrown puzzle pieces everywhere. The only things I understood were that he was going home and that I would be left hanging. I wanted to be able to hug him, and tell him how worried I was. But I couldn't, so I wrote,

I worry about you.

I know you do. Thank you. That means a lot to me.

Be careful, okay? I knew things would be different now—that this assignment was much more important than he'd let on. *You*

better get a good night's sleep. We can talk tomorrow when you get back. I'll wait up for you.

Sure. The email explains a lot of things I want you to know. And I'd like to exchange addresses, if you're okay with that.

I'd really like that. I paused, then wrote for the first time, *I love you, my friend.*

He didn't answer me right away. I thought he'd signed off, but then I saw it.

Love you too. And thank you for always being here for me.

Hey, it's a hard job, but someone has to do it.

I tried to make it light and funny, but it didn't quite come out that way. It was as if he was saying goodbye to me, and I didn't know how to respond.

Want another dream to take with you?

Nawh, think I'll pass this time.

Okay.

Now I was disappointed and very worried. He never passed up a dream.

Well, this soldier is feeling tired.

I'll keep you close to my heart until we talk again.

Night.

Something just wasn't right about this assignment. My soldier was feeling the same way too; I could tell from our conversation. He was scared in a way that he'd never been before. He'd been depressed and confused, but never scared.

163

CHAPTER 26
THE ASSIGNMENT

The morning was gray and rainy.

"Damn rain!" he cursed. "One more assignment, and I'll be out of here."

Stuffing the last piece of equipment into his backpack, he slung it over his shoulder. He took one last look around his hut, as if he saying goodbye to it. Then he headed outside, where his troop was waiting for him.

The chopper was just warming up. The blades whispered in a rhythmic voice, "Be careful. Be careful." He'd lied to the stranger about the briefing. In fact, the urgency of it told him that it was more dangerous than any other assignment he'd ever been on. His men were understandably edgy.

"Okay men, listen up. Here're our orders: We're going into Russian territory. Special ops."

His men looked at each other. He could see the fear in their eyes. They'd also sensed the danger.

He continued with a steady voice. "We have to check on a camp there. No fighting. Just get in, photograph it—without the enemy discovering us—and get the hell out. Bring the pictures

164

back here, and we're done. The chopper will drop us at our coordinates. And after we've completed the assignment, we'll radio it to pick us up." Simple and easy. "I don't want any heroics or stupidity. Just follow my orders. And when it's finished, we go home. Merry Christmas, men."

He smiled at his troop. It was a strained smile, but he wanted to ease their fears.

"Back to the States? This soon?" asked Browning.

The troop was buzzing.

"We ship out immediately after we return from our assignment. They'll fly us to Germany, where we'll get our release orders. Then we head home to the States." He walked up and down the row of young soldiers. "So be extra careful today. Don't want to lose any of you guys. Kinda gotten used to you all."

He chuckled.

"Yes sir!" His men stood at attention to show their respect for him. They'd been in Kosovo long enough. They were all tired and needed the comfort of their loved ones.

The chopper ride was bumpy, but he kept reviewing the orders and maps with his men. He wanted to make sure they all knew their part in the assignment. The chopper flew low over the treetops until it came to a small field. As they neared the landing area, Sarge gave the orders.

"Stay alert. Let's do this right, and get home fast!" he barked, trying to sound confident.

The chopper landed in the long, willowy grasses of a meadow. To the right there was a dense, vast forest.

"When I give the order, head to the trees for cover."

The helicopter doors opened. The men anticipated the order. Finally, it arrived.

"Go!"

One by one, they jumped to the ground and headed to the thick terrain for cover. Once safely in the forest, Sarge looked back. The chopper took off with a blast of air, leaving them alone in the unknown.

Sarge motioned for them to move out.

The troop plunged steadily through the thickness of the entangled trees and the narrow passes along the gullies. They stayed off any beaten paths, so they wouldn't be seen by the enemy soldiers. Pushing upward through the rough terrain of the mountainous area, they only stopped long enough to check their compasses and make sure they were headed in the right direction.

The forest was eerie. There was nothing but the sound of twigs breaking, the rain falling, and a few grunts from the men as the branches slashed back at them. The cold seemed to permeate everything as the troop pressed onward.

Their orders were to make their way to a safe haven, take refuge, and wait for nightfall. Under the cloak of night, they'd slip into the enemy zone, get a headcount of the prisoners, record the layout of the camp, and get out of there as quickly as they could without being seen.

No fighting, thought Sarge. *It's easy: just get in and get out.* But he knew it wouldn't be that simple. The enemy couldn't even know they were there. He didn't have any idea how large the camp was, or how many enemy soldiers it contained.

He hadn't told his men, but there was one more thing he had to do once they arrived. He'd decided that he wouldn't share this information until the right moment. He wasn't sure if he'd make it out alive.

In a single-file line, they silently made their way up and through the rough terrain of the mountainous forest. The camp seemed further away than he'd been told. The rugged steps and thick foliage were hard to traverse. It was taking far longer than it was supposed to.

Sarge raised his hand and motioned to stop. "Take a ten-minute break. Then we have to move faster. We're not making good time."

He dropped his pack on the ground and grabbed his canteen. *I could sure use a stronger drink right now*, he thought to himself. Then he changed his mind. *When I get back home, I have to stop all this drinking, for Catherine. It's not good.*

He looked at his troop resting, and he could tell they were nervous.

"Let's move out!" he barked. He picked up his pack and slung it over his back.

After a few more hours, he motioned for his men to stop. He looked around to make sure they were all together. "Okay, this is it. We're near the camp, so we'll rest here until it's dark. Then we'll move in."

It was raining harder, and they were tired from hiking. And they needed their energy for what was ahead.

Just get in and get out, he kept reminding himself. *Just get in and get out.*

Night fell fast, and it stopped raining. Gathering his men, he once again reviewed his orders to make sure they understood. "We're near the enemy camp, so move slowly and quietly. We need to remain *unnoticed*. Got it?"

"Yes sir."

They were in unknown territory, so the enemy had the advantage.

His men were somber and silent as they blackened their faces and picked up their packs, ready to move. After a few miles of tracking through the thick brush, he saw lights ahead.

Once again, Sarge silently motioned for them to stop.

Dropping to his belly, he crawled up onto the ridge that overlooked the camp and took out his binoculars. Scanning the camp, he realized that there were more enemy soldiers than he'd been briefed about.

We've gone this far, he thought. *But we have to be careful.*

Calling Browning and Thompson over to him, he motioned for the rest of the men to take position. They checked their ammunition and quickly dispersed.

"Browning?"

"Yes sir?"

"Stay with me, okay? Watch my back."

"Yes sir." Browning moved in closer to Sarge, proud that his C.O. trusted him to watch his back.

"Thompson?"

"Yes sir?"

"You got your camera ready?"

"Yes sir."

"I want you to get as close as you can to take your shots. Once we hit camp, we need pictures of the huts and the prisoners. Make sure they're good; I don't want to have to come back. Got it?"

"Yes sir."

Thompson checked his camera and made sure it was ready to go.

With his back turned to Thompson, Sarge also checked his own camera, just in case. Then he moved quietly over to the other men, who were waiting for their orders. He could feel adrenaline flowing through his veins.

He called three names: "Stevens, Adams, Smith."

"Here sir." The three young men moved closer to their sergeant, waiting for their orders.

"You head down the hill and check out how many guards

there are. Find out where they're located, so we can figure out the best way to enter the camp."

"Yes sir."

"The rest of you are to wait here until we get back." He searched their faces. "Remain quiet and bide your time. I don't want to hear a peep from any of you. That means no gunshots unless I give the order. You got that?" He paused. "If we aren't back at the designated time, then head for the chopper, and get the hell out of here."

The men looked at him. He could smell their fear.

"But sir—"

He interrupted. "I don't want any of you playing hero. You got me?" His voice was calm and gruff, which affirmed his authority.

"Yes sir."

"No heroics!"

They didn't like that order.

"Set your watches, and let's head out."

The men stationed themselves, ready for a fight. The night was pitch-black as they headed to the core of the enemy camp.

No moon tonight. That's in our favor, thought Sarge as he crawled silently toward the confines of the camp. He silently prayed that they'd go unnoticed.

Stevens, Adams, and Smith headed out to count the guards and determine their positions. When they got back, they reported what they'd seen. There were three towers, each with guards with machine guns. There was a double barbed wire fence, with a trench just inside of it. And inside the trench, there were some huts. There was a large hut to the right, which was probably the headquarters, and a few small huts to the left.

"Since the prisoners are indoors, we have to sneak inside the camp. So that means we should have fifteen minutes until the guards change out."

"And there're two guards with dogs walking the perimeter of the camp," Stevens relayed.

"Dogs? Damn! Wasn't expecting dogs." Sarge checked the direction of the wind. "It should be okay. The north wind is moving pretty fast, so the dogs might not pick up our smell."

Nothing was the way it was supposed to be. He cursed.

They moved closer, so Sarge could watch the movement of the guards with his own eyes. Soon, the guard in the tower closest to them started his switchover. *At least that's going as predicted*, he thought.

When all of the dogs were away from the spot in the barbed wire he was eyeing, they moved in. They only had a few minutes before they'd be within eyesight of a guard. Luckily, his men were fast at cutting the barbed wire. Stevens, Adams, and Smith headed back to take their positions with the rest of the troop.

One by one, Browning, Thompson, and Sarge slithered under the barbed wire and through the trench to the bowels of the camp. Quietly they made their way to one of the smaller huts. Looking through the cracks of the wood, Sarge could see the prisoners. He nodded to Thompson, and they focused their cameras and took some shots of them.

Sarge gasped at the condition of the prisoners. Men were lying on the damp, cold ground. Some of them had broken bones sticking out of their skin. Others had dark bruises, burns, and torture marks. They were undernourished and sick — coughing and moaning. Their eyes were sunken into their faces, and purple bags hung below the empty crevasses that had once danced with happiness.

He wanted to help them escape, but his orders were to get in and get out. He was just supposed to get pictures. Now more than ever, he didn't agree with these orders or the war. But he'd signed up to protect his country, and he knew he had to follow orders. But he didn't have to like them.

"Twelve, thirteen, fourteen," he continued counting to himself. Then he turned to Browning and whispered, "Fourteen in total. Remember that number, just in case I don't make it."

Browning nodded and readied his gun for any surprises. Satisfied that they had enough pictures, they headed over to the next small hut. Again there was the stench of death and defecation, which made the men nauseous. After a full count of the prisoners and sufficient pictures were taken, he gave Thompson and Browning orders.

Now was the time to break the news.

"Stay put. I'm heading over to the larger hut. I have orders. If I'm not back in twenty minutes, then leave without me. Join the other men, and head to the meadow."

"I'll come with you, Sarge," stated Browning.

"No, you will stay here."

"I can help you."

"I said NO! That's an order."

Browning backed down. He and Thompson slipped quietly from building to building, unnoticed by the guards. Once close to the barbed wire confinements, they stooped down and took cover.

The large hut was more dangerous to get to, but he had his orders. Sarge nodded to his men and headed out alone, slithering on his belly. His elbows were aching from the effort of crawling, and his heart was hammering loudly in his chest. He thought that the enemy would definitely hear it.

Passing the ammunition and supply huts, he finally made it to the larger hut. He crept around to the back and peered through the cracks of the rough wooden planks. It was in fact the main hut, where the enemy kept their plans and radio equipment. A soldier was sitting at the desk in the middle of the room doing paperwork.

One man, he considered. *Easier than I thought it would be.*

After a few minutes, the enemy soldier left the room and went outside for a smoke. Sarge could hear him speaking to another soldier on the porch. He quietly made his way around to the side of the hut, where there was a window. Holding his camera still, he slipped through the open window and walked over to the desk. Shuffling through the maps and papers, he couldn't find what he'd been sent for.

Looking around the room, he spotted a filing cabinet. Quietly he crossed the room and eased the top drawer open. Scanning the files, he pulled one out labeled "Confidential." Opening it, he realized it was what he'd come for.

Spreading the papers out, he quickly took pictures of all the information that was inside the file. Sarge's heart was beating so hard that his chest hurt. He couldn't make out the difference between the returning footsteps on the old wooden porch and the pounding of his heart. Quickly he pushed the file back in its place and closed the drawer.

The enemy soldier was almost to the door.

Sarge cursed as he moved to the far side of the filing cabinet. He squatted down and pushed his body as close to the wall as he could. Holding his breath, he waited.

The doorknob turned, and the enemy soldier stepped inside. But his friend called to him, so he turned and went back outside.

Sarge slipped his camera into his pocket and quickly headed across the room to the window. Turning to make sure that no one had seen him, he spotted a piece of paper on the floor next to the filing cabinet, but he wasn't sure how long it'd been there. He started to dart back across room, but the doorknob was turning again.

His men were anxiously waiting across the yard. Trying to calm his breathing, he realized just how close the encounter had been. The enemy soldier sat down at his desk and continued his paperwork. The intrusion had gone unnoticed.

Once again he slithered across the yard to the perimeter of the camp, where Browning and Thompson were hiding. Browning looked at Sarge questioningly, but he couldn't tell him what he'd done. For that matter, he couldn't tell anyone. They made their way through the trench and under the barbed wire fences, then disappeared into the unpredictable night.

The rest of the troop sat waiting, alert to the noises of the forest. The bushes crackled, so they readied their rifles. The men breathed a sigh of relief when they saw Sarge and the others. And they were even more relieved when he motioned for them to quickly head back to their point of destination.

CHAPTER 27
THE POUNDING HEART

Abruptly sitting up in bed, she clutched her heart as it pounded deeply in her chest. Something wasn't right; she could feel it. Slipping out of bed, she rushed to the computer. Nothing.

Still, she had this pummeling feeling. What if something had happened to her Stone Soldier? After all he'd been through.... She didn't want to think about what might have happened. To change her train of thought, she went to the stove to turn on the kettle. "A hot cup of tea will help me calm down." She reprimanded herself for being so silly. She was just worried because her soldier was on a dangerous mission.

"That's what it is. I'm just overreacting." She took her tea into the front room and sat in her big, overstuffed chair. "Everything is fine. He'll be just fine." She said a silent prayer for her Stone Soldier and hoped that her premonitions were wrong.

CHAPTER 28
THE BATTLE

"What was that all about, Sarge?" Browning asked, trying to catch up with him.

"Nothing," Sarge answered offishly.

"You almost got caught, didn't you?"

"I said it was nothing!" Sarge snapped, knowing that he couldn't divulge his mission. Browning looked hurt, but Sarge couldn't care. All he could care about at that moment was getting his men back to the safety of the helicopter. Quickly they climbed over the jagged rocks, groped through the thick, entangled forest, and pushed forward towards the meadow.

Just ahead of them voices could be heard. Sarge motioned for his men to take cover. Slouching down like cats, they made themselves as difficult to shoot as possible and readied their guns.

Anticipation grew during the silence. The voices got closer and louder. Once again, Sarge silently motioned for his men to stay quiet, hoping that the enemy soldiers would pass by without discovering them.

The two enemy soldiers stopped right next to the spot where the troop had taken cover. Then they sat down on a fallen log that

175

was inches away from Browning's position in the foliage. Sarge looked at Browning, giving him a silent order to maintain his position. Aiming his gun at the enemy, he waited. After about ten minutes, the two men continued on their way.

One of his men leaned back, and a twig snapped. The two enemy soldiers stopped, turned around, aimed their guns, and listened. Finally, they seemingly decided it was nothing and continued on their way. After he was sure they were out of earshot, Sarge gave the order to continue down the savage, mountainous terrain.

Dawn was overcoming the night, and the fog was rolling in thick, making the pathway hard to follow. After about an hour of hiking down the pathway, Sarge motioned for his troop to stop. Something wasn't right.

His body became stiff with fear as he realized what it was.

The two soldiers they'd seen earlier hadn't just been making rounds. They were rejoining an entire battalion that was hunting his small troop. The enemy soldier in the large hut must've discovered the piece of paper he'd dropped.

He could hear the faint sound of enemy soldiers in the distance. From the sounds of things, there were a lot of them. He motioned for his troop to take cover and ready themselves for the brunt of the enemy battalion's attack. The helplessness of the situation engulfed him.

He closed his eyes, trying to control his breathing. "Dear God, please let my men stay safe."

He considered how this prayer might manifest itself. "Too far to go to reach the meadow. Maybe they'll turn back." He hoped that the helicopter had already landed. Then the enemy soldiers wouldn't hear it.

His men looked at him with fear and terror in their eyes. They'd been in dangerous situations before, but nothing like this one. They were so outnumbered. He knew their lives were in his hands. He had to get them off this mountain. His sweaty fingers shook as he clasped the algid steel of his weapon and tried to make visual contact. He knew they were in a tight spot and might not be able to avert the consequences that'd follow.

Then gunfire rang out. They were under attack.

The forest was being saturated by morning light. Screams and moans echoed in the foggy mist as brief glimpses of dark forms moved among the trees and foliage. His men kept firing into the enemy. He couldn't tell the difference between his men and the enemy soldiers. Worn down by the turmoil of battle, the enemy slowly moved back. But were they retreating or regrouping?

Either way, Sarge gave the order to move out. His men were running as fast as they could, stumbling over branches and dead logs. Finding a well-worn path, they followed it down the mountain. Sarge was thankful that the descent was easier than the ascent had been. His troop quickly made their way down the path toward the meadow.

Behind them, Sarge could hear the enemy closing in again. He motioned for a couple of his soldiers to stay behind and take defensive positions along either side of the pathway. When they could see the enemy soldiers, Sarge's men looked over at him for the signal. He finally gave it, and they hurled grenades into the middle of the enemy battalion. Eventually the enemy soldiers withdrew. Sarge yelled for them to move out. He mustered all the strength he could as he ran down the path.

The troop resumed its rapid tread through the forest. Once they reached the summit, they knew that safety was nearby. They were on the final leg of the journey.

It wasn't supposed to be like this, he thought. *This wasn't the plan. We're supposed to go home, not die here.*

He could only pray that they would make it to the meadow,

and that the helicopter would be there. But he knew that when the fog lifted, they wouldn't stand a chance. Then out of nowhere, a flare lit up the sky like the Fourth of July. His pupils dilated with the intensity of his gaze. The enemy battalion's position had been revealed.

Gun at the ready, he searched the murky haze for his prey. They had no choice but to open fire and hope for the best. Sarge said a silent prayer, took a deep breath, and gave the order to fire.

Suddenly, an enemy soldier jumped out from behind a tree and lunged toward him, causing him to drop his gun. Reaching down, he pulled out his knife and viciously shoved it into the enemy soldier's chest. Blood poured mercilessly out of the deep wound and spewed across his shirt. The enemy soldier dropped to his knees and let out a moan.

Sarge released him and he dropped to the ground, ashen and lifeless. Looking down, he saw his blood-stained hands. He tried to wipe the blood off on his shirt, but it wouldn't go away. Then he realized that he'd been wounded in the fight.

Now that the other enemy soldiers had been wounded enough to significantly slow them down, he struggled to give a roll call. "Browning?"

"Here," came a shaky voice behind him.

"Thompson?"

"Here, Sarge."

"Get on the radio, and get us some reinforcements out here fast."

"Yes sir," replied Thompson.

"Stevens?"

"My arm got hit bad, Sarge. Shrapnel in my shoulder.... Can't use it."

"Adams?" No response. "You hit?"

"Yep, pretty bad, Sarge," Adams finally replied.

"You okay to make it down the mountain?"

"Need some help, Sarge. Sorry."

"It's okay, kid." Sarge swore. "Smith, give Adams a hand."

Smith crawled over to where Adams was laying.

After Sarge knew all the details of the wounded, he gave orders about heading down the mountain as quickly as possible. Day was breaking, and the fog was lifting. They needed to make it to the meadow before the enemy could attack again.

When the men heard the chopper approaching overhead, they quickened their pace. As Sarge wiped the sweat off his forehead, blood dripped down his arm. He was hit pretty badly, but he knew he had to keep going, wounded or not.

"Hold up. Rest for a minute," he whispered to Browning in a weak voice. He collapsed to the ground amid the ambiguity of the woods. His head was spinning as he felt the adrenaline fading from his body. He listened for the enemy. He couldn't hear them — only the sound of the chopper getting closer.

He stood up, using his rifle to support him. His chest and head felt like he'd been hit with a cannon.

"Move out! The chopper is waiting," he barked with authority. He tried to walk, but each step was too painful. "Hurry! Faster!"

Browning grabbed Sarge under his arm to help support him. His men grabbed the wounded and headed down the last lag of the hill. The beating of the chopper blades was getting closer.

They were moving faster now, over logs and through the deep darkness of the woods. Suddenly, Sarge tripped over a branch that was sticking up in the pathway. He heard his leg snap, and he fell.

He cursed as the pain ripped through him. Browning tried to help him stand, but the pain was too much. His leg wouldn't hold him. Examining his leg, he saw the gristle of the bone sticking out. There was blood everywhere.

The panic on Browning's face made him realize how dire the situation was.

"Not so good, Browning?" He tried to force a laugh, but the pain was overwhelming.

Browning's eyes grew large as he looked at his sergeant's leg.

"Not good at all." Sarge faintly answered his own question.

***

Browning ripped off a piece of his shirt and tied it tightly around Sarge's leg to stop the bleeding. "Okay, you hold on to me—I'll get you down the hill."

Browning pulled him up and tried to carry him on his shoulder. Sarge let out a blood-curdling scream. Browning put him back down and looked at him.

"You've been shot too?" Browning had come to love Sarge.

"Naah, just grazed." Blood was trickling down his forehead.

"You got shot in the head!" Browning tried to wipe away the blood. The troop had stopped and turned in the pathway, waiting for them to catch up.

Sarge smiled. He actually didn't know he'd been shot. In fact, he wasn't feeling much of anything at that moment.

"Still here, ain't I?" He laughed, then coughed. Red liquid trickled from his mouth.

"I'm gonna get you out of this mess, Sarge." Browning started to pull him up again, but the pain was too much.

***

"No good, Browning. You better get going. Get everyone back to the helicopter. Leave me. I'll try to follow." He waved for Browning to leave him alone.

"What do you mean, Sarge?" Browning was panicking now.

"Just leave me. I'll be okay. Just head down the hill with the men. Here, take my camera back with you." He coughed up more blood and handed him his camera.

180

Browning cursed. "You're in a bad way, Sarge."

"That's an order, Browning. Didn't you hear me? Take the men, and head down that hill." His voice was sharp and demanding. He was the Stone Soldier once again.

"No, I can't leave you here, sir."

"Can't you take an order?" Sarge's voice was weak. "You're in charge now. The men's lives are in your hands."

Browning was shaking. "Yes sir!"

Thompson came running over to them. "Gotta go now, Sarge. The enemy soldiers are coming back. We can hear them through the bushes. The chopper is waiting." Then he saw Sarge and couldn't believe the mutilated mess he was looking at. He was in shock. "What the hell happened? He's all shot up. Damn, look at his leg." Thompson addressed Browning. "We gotta go! Give me a hand. We can carry him to the chopper."

Only half-unconscious from the loss of blood, Sarge looked up the pathway, then back down the slope that led to the chopper. He could hear the enemy soldiers in the distance.

***

"Sarge? We gotta go now!" Browning didn't want to leave him there, but he knew he had to take the order.

Thompson looked at Browning, "What should we do?"

"How the hell would I know?"

"Browning, the enemy is getting close." Thompson waited for an answer that Browning didn't seem to have. He punched Browning on the arm. "Did you hear me? I said we have to go!"

Sarge reached up and grabbed Browning's arm. "Put me over there in the bush behind the log."

Browning and Thompson obeyed.

Sarge reached for his gun, then checked his ammunition. "Got any more ammo, Browning? I seem to be low." He was fading again.

181

Browning dug into this pouch and gave him the rest of his ammunition, "That's all I got, sir."

"That's enough, Browning. I'm gonna kill those sons of...." His voice trailed off as he lost consciousness.

"I'll come back for you, Sarge." Browning's voice had softened. "I promise I'll come back for you."

The other men were anxiously waiting a little further down the path. Browning gave them Sarge's order.

"You can't just leave him there," Stevens refuted.

"I said I got my orders. If we don't go now, the helicopter will leave. Now move out!" Browning barked.

The young soldiers knew exactly what was going to happen. They had come to love their sergeant, but there was nothing they could do. Begrudgingly they headed down the pathway.

"Be damned lucky if we get out of here alive." Browning cursed.

The sun shook from the folds of morning, making the pathway clearer and easier to maneuver. They could see the chopper now. Its blades chanted, "Faster, faster, faster." Rushing from the shelter of the forest, they climbed into the chopper.

Browning looked back toward the place where they'd left Sarge, then gave the order to take off.

CHAPTER 29
THE EMAIL

That morning I'd checked my email, and there it was—just as he'd promised.

I was shaking. I wanted to know who Christopher was, but I was afraid to open the email. For a long time, I sat looking at the screen. Then I reached over and clicked the mouse.

My dearest friend:

"There is nothing more dear in life than the thoughts and wishes of a real friend." — My Grandmother

I feel that you are truly a cherished friend.

So many times, I've been at the end of my rope. So many times, I wanted to give up.

Then you came into my life, and everything changed. You cared. You reached out to a perfect stranger and gave me a deep, wonderful friendship. Now I realize how lucky I was to have met you. Because of this friendship, my life has changed. You taught me to treasure the beauty of life, and to enjoy being in the moment. You taught me to love myself, to love my life, and to love the things that I've been given.

Because of all this, I feel I need to share the darkest part of my life with you. I owe it to you. So tonight, I'm going to tell you about my past — how I ended up here.

I'm going home soon, and when I do, I'll always remember the lessons you've taught me. I won't run away from those who love and care for me anymore. I'll always try to keep this lesson close to my heart.

When I get back from my assignment, I'd like to exchange names. And if you'll allow it, I'd love to meet you.

I hope you'll understand where my heart has been, and forgive me. It happened on the night of my father's 60th birthday party....

CHAPTER 30
THE RECALL

The Stone Soldier reached into his pocket and pulled out the picture of Christopher. The blood ran down his arm to his hand, covering the photo. He wiped it off and smiled.

He thought about his parents and little Catherine. He thought about how he would never see her again. He thought about how much he regretted losing a life that felt like a beautiful dream.

When blood dripped on the picture again, he remembered the last time his arm had bled like this. It was the night of the accident.

The helplessness of the situation.... The limpness of his body.... The depth of his pain....

It all caused his mind to wander back in time to the moment when....

***

He was standing in the cold darkness of the house. It had been a long night. Too long. Everything felt like a movie, but someone had written the script all wrong. Tossing his coat on the chair by the kitchen table, he walked over to the cupboard and reached in. His hand clumsily searched around.

He swore quietly, so he wouldn't wake up the baby. He walked into the hallway and over to the chair, where Christopher always left Catherine's little pink blanket. But it wasn't there. He ran his hand over the top of the chair.

Then he remembered that his mother had wrapped Catherine in the blanket, kissed him, and taken Catherine for the night. She felt it was better that way. She muttered something about him needing to take some time for himself and think. Think? That was exactly what he didn't want to do.

Nevertheless, she took Catherine with her and said she'd call in the morning. When she left that night, she had no idea how long she'd be taking care of her granddaughter.

The house was too quiet. There was nothing but the sound of darkness. As he walked into the kitchen and over to the cupboard, the sound felt deafening. Opening the door, he impatiently pushed the items around until they spewed out, hitting the black-and-white tile.

He cursed again, pushing his arm further into the cupboard. "I know it's there. I haven't touched it since last Christmas."

Finally, his hand found what he was looking for: a smooth, tall bottle. Placing it on the counter, he picked up a dirty glass from the sink, opened the bottle, and poured out a little of the dark amber liquid. Closing his eyes, he swallowed hard. But the burning sensation only numbed his mind for a moment.

So again, he reached for the bottle. This time, he poured until the glass was full. Pausing a moment to calm the sick feeling that was overtaking him, he looked at the glass, contemplated the effect, and angrily tossed the glass across the kitchen. The shattering noise echoed loudly.

He picked up the bottle and walked outside onto the patio. Slumping down into the deck chair, he put the bottle to his lips and gulped deeply. He waited for the feeling he needed. He wanted the memories of the night to burn away, but they were still there — vivid and cold.

The phone rang — once, twice, three times. Then it stopped. It rang again. He ignored it. Christopher's voice cheerfully filled up the absence in the house. "Hi, my family and I are busy at the moment. Please leave a message." Then a soft giggle followed.

"Christopher?" he called into the darkness. Peter expected to see him standing in the doorway, but he wasn't there. There was nothing but the empty darkness.

"Christopher?" His voice once again recoiled in the dead hollowness of the night.

He sat, listening for a reply. Finally he heard someone crying in the night. Then he limply dropped his head into his hands; he'd recognized the voice as his own. A heavy dampness wrapped itself around him like a python, squeezing tightly.

He looked up at the stars. Christopher loved the stars.

***

"See." Christopher pointed to the sky. "See, over there."

"Where?" Peter couldn't tell which ones Christopher was looking at.

"Over there." Christopher pointed again.

"Over where?" he whispered in a gruff voice as he snuggled closer to him.

"To the right, silly."

"I'd rather be doing this." Peter began kissing Christopher, pulling him closer to him.

"Okay, be serious. Follow my hand, and you'll see the Big Dipper. Then look a little to the right." Christopher's hand dropped to his side as Peter pulled him close to him. "Stop fooling around. I'm trying to teach you something."

"Now, how can I concentrate when you're around?"

Christopher laughed, pushed himself away from him, and

187

darted down toward the river.

"Christopher, you know you love it as much as I do," he called after him.

Christopher sat on the plush green grass at the edge of the river, and Peter quietly sat beside him. Peter loved him and couldn't comprehend living even one day without him. Christopher turned and smiled at him, his eyes dancing with mischief in the moonlight.

"How lucky can a guy be?" he murmured as he buried his face in his wavy hair.

"What?"

"Nothing."

Christopher giggled and cuddled into him. They sat on the edge of the river for a long time, enjoying the silence of the stars together.

***

Still gazing at the sky, he cried, "Why? Why?"

A gurgling sound escaped his throat. He lowered his head back into the security of his large, calloused hands.

His voice trailed off as he waited for the answer to his question. Time stood still in the hands of the night. The pain and agony whittled away inside him. Weak and exhausted, he walked back into the house, and momentarily stood in the archway leading into the kitchen. Then he continued upstairs.

In the bedroom, the chiffon curtains lightly waved in the breeze. He shivered. The flowers in the wallpaper delicately danced under the moonlight, and the white of the comforter shone like the purity of snow on a young winter's night. A slight whiff of sweet geraniums and sandalwood hung lightly in the air. He breathed in deeply, allowing the scent to comfort him.

***

"Aren't you ready yet?" he asked him.

"As my mother used to say, 'I don't wake up looking my best.'"

Christopher was still shirtless, leaving the darkness of his skin beckoning to be touched. Peter bent over and tenderly kissed the nape of his neck. Christopher giggled and melted into Peter's strong masculine form.

"I love you," he whispered in Christopher's ear, gently kissing his cheeks. He moved slowly to his eyes and nose, then passionately placed his lips on his. Christopher kissed him back, leaving him feeling a love that he never thought he'd experience. He pulled him closer and kissed him with a deeper urgency. Christopher pulled away and smiled at him, his lips teasing Peter's.

"We can't, Pete. We'll be late for the party."

Once again he reached for Christopher, but he gently pulled further away.

"Forget their party. We'll have our own."

"No, I promised your mother that I would get there early to help her get ready for her guests, and it's already getting late. She'll be livid if I'm not there." Gently, Christopher placed his finger against the fullness of his own lips, then placed it on Peter's lips. "Tonight," Christopher promised.

"Then I'll have to leave the room, because I don't want to be responsible for what I'll do to you."

Christopher picked up his hair gel and threw it at him. He jumped out of the way, slipping quickly through the doorway and into the hall.

***

Turning on the bathroom tap, he bent down and submerged his head under the cold water. Reaching for the towel that was perfectly folded beside the sink, he gazed into the mirror. Sweat was pouring off his deeply tanned skin, but he didn't recognize

189

the face that was staring back at him.

He stumbled over to the bed and fell onto it in exhaustion. Sleep overcame him for the moment.

***

"Christopher, that was Ma on the phone," he called from the bottom of the stairs. "Christopher?"

Then Christopher appeared at the top of the stairs. When there was a special occasion like this, he was always surprised by how attracted to Christopher he still was. Their friends teased them about their love, but he didn't mind. He knew they'd found something very unique — deeper and stronger than the love of other couples.

He whistled. Christopher smiled and blushed.

"Well, you look very handsome."

"You know I fall in love with you more and more each day."

Peter raised his hand and traced the line of Christopher's neck, working his way slowly down his arm. He brushed Christopher's lips softly against his. "Me too, Kit. Me too."

The phone rang again.

"Are you going to answer that?" Christopher asked.

"I just want to remember this moment," Peter mumbled.

"It's probably your mother again. You're better at dealing with her than me."

After a short conversation, he hung up the phone. "That was the sitter. She's going to be late."

Christopher looked at him, worried. "We're going to be terribly late, and I promised your mother...."

"That's okay. You take the car and go ahead. Mother will be frantic if you don't. I can leave when the sitter arrives. Then we can drive home together, and pick up my truck tomorrow. No problem."

"Okay.... Do you think we should take Catherine with us,

and forget about the sitter?"

"She's been sick."

"We could just stay here."

He kissed Christopher on the forehead. "It'll be just fine."

"Yes, you're right." But he still looked worried. "I just hate rearranging things. You know me."

He kissed him again. "If you don't leave now, Mother will be sending the police to see why we aren't there yet."

Christopher laughed, and the strain finally escaped his face. "She's not that bad!"

The phone rang yet again. They both looked at it and laughed. Christopher turned to pick up his coat and umbrella from the chair by the stairwell. Catherine's little pink blanket was on the back of the chair. Christopher ran his hand across it, then worriedly added, "Don't forget to give the sitter your mother's telephone number in case she needs us. And our cell numbers are on the fridge. The doctor's number is on the —"

"Christopher, stop worrying."

"The bottle is in the fridge, and Catherine should have it at 8:00. Then she should go back to sleep. If there are any problems —"

"I know, I know, phone my mother's house right away."

"Oh, you're making fun of me, Petey." Christopher bent forward and kissed him sweetly. "It's just that the sitter is new, and I —"

"Let's just have a good time tonight."

Opening the door, Christopher raced out. "See you there, sweetheart."

"Drive carefully. You know what it's like on Saturday night. People are crazy."

He stood in the doorway and watched as Christopher drove away, then headed upstairs to get his shoes and jacket.

191

It was his father's sixtieth birthday, and his mother had planned a huge party for him. Everyone was going to be there.

Christopher had spent the last few nights taking care of Catherine. They'd talked about not going, but his mother would never forgive them. Besides, Christopher needed a night out, and Catherine seemed so much better that day.

The sitter kept him waiting longer than she'd said she would on the phone. *Not a good sign*, he thought. Finally, she arrived. He showed her around the house, told her where the emergency numbers were, and gave her Catherine's schedule.

Turning towards the stairway, he took the sitter up into the nursery where Catherine was sleeping. One again, he stressed the importance of calling them if Catherine wasn't feeling well. He bent over the crib, gently kissed Catherine good night, and headed out to the party.

***

"If only we'd taken Catherine with us like Christopher wanted. She wasn't even sick anymore. Why did I have to pick that night to be our date night?" He tossed and turned in bed. "If only we'd stayed home like he suggested."

His body was contorted in guilt. The bed seemed so empty now. Finally, he got up and went downstairs to the den. Lying on the couch, he meticulously went over all the details of the night.

"If only…." The blame came hard and heavy, hitting him like a hammer.

"If only…."

CHAPTER 31
THE FIXATION

My phone was ringing, and the timer was going off on the oven. But I couldn't move. My soldier was revealing the darkest moment of his life to me, and I was glued to the screen.

I was finally able to see some truths through the layers of mystery.

He's gay. He was married to a man named Christopher, and Catherine is their daughter.

Yet he seemed as accepting of his sexual orientation as I was. That being the case, what had caused him to become such a tortured soul?

Chapter 32
The Rainstorm

It was darker than usual that night as he drove toward his parents' house. The wind had picked up, and the rain was falling hard and fast. The traffic was heavy, but he knew it would thin out when he turned off the main road.

Turning onto the connecting road, he saw the flashing lights of police cars, fire trucks, and ambulances. Everyone in front of him slowed down as they neared the accident.

He cursed. He was late enough as it was. Christopher would think there was something wrong with Catherine. Reaching into his pocket for his cell phone, he realized he'd forgotten it.

He cursed again. The car in front of him came to a stop.

Now what? he thought impatiently. He turned on the radio to see if he could hear an update about the accident. Reaching into his jacket pocket, he pulled out a cigarette and lit it. Exhaling, he leaned back in the seat to relax. *Looks like it's going to be awhile.* Seeing the clock on the dashboard, he got edgy about the delay again. *Christopher will be worried about me.*

The cars started moving slowly. He put the truck in gear and slowly inched up. But people were as morbidly curious as ever. Everyone had to have a look, so it slowed the traffic down. Stopping and starting. Waiting. He hated it when people were curious about accidents. "Just get on with your business, and leave it to the police. They know what they're doing."

Finally, the traffic started to move faster. As he neared the accident, his heart jumped. Three vehicles: A semi-truck, a blue ford van, and….

His skin crawled. It couldn't be. He reached his head as far forward as possible, trying to make out the license plate number. He wiped the condensation from the glass. Then he rolled down the window and leaned out. It was raining even harder than when he'd left, so visibility was bad.

The red car was demolished, crushed like an accordion. It had been in the middle of the two vehicles. There was almost nothing left of it. As he neared the site of the accident, the sick feeling in his stomach worsened. He could finally see the numbers on the license plate.

"Oh God!" His heart stopped.

He frantically stopped his truck, opened the door, and stepped out. Not bothering to shut the door, he just left his truck sitting in the middle of the road and recklessly darted through traffic toward the red car. The other cars were impatiently honking at him.

A police officer came running toward him. "You have to move your car. We need to keep the road clear."

"I don't care." He was pushing forward to the mutilated heap of metal that sat in the middle of the road.

"Sir, you can't go in there." The police officer tried to physically restrain him.

"Leave me the hell alone!" he shouted, and wrenched his arm from the grip of the young officer.

"Charlie," the officer said into his CB. "Get over here. I need help."

Another officer came running toward them. Dodging both of the men, he ran toward the wreckage. Cars were honking and people were shouting, but he didn't care. He needed to get to the car. He needed to know.

He pulled at the driver's door.

"Sir, you need to get out of here. The Jaws of Life are coming. You have to move. They need to—"

"Christopher!" he screamed as he tugged at the metal. "Christopher!"

He was frantic. The nausea was overwhelming, and he felt like someone had hit him hard in the head. Everyone was pulling at him.

"Get your hands off me!"

"Sir." Charlie, the older officer, firmly pulled him away from the car.

He heard Christopher moan weakly.

"Get him out of there!" He dropped to his knees and tried to reach into the car. "He's my husband! God damn you all!"

They all looked at each other in shock. Jumping up, he hurriedly looked around. Spotting an axe hanging on the side of a fire truck, he ran over to it, grabbed it, and ran back to the car.

The officers held him down, but he struggled against them. Wrenching the axe from him, an officer said, "You aren't helping him this way. You need to calm down. The Jaws of Life will get him out, but in the meantime, you need to calm down for your partner's sake. You need to move away from the car and let everyone do their jobs."

His heart sank. The helplessness of the situation finally hit him. He could forget he wasn't legally married until a stranger reminded him. His body felt limp and weak.

"You have to help him." He dropped to his knees in anguish.

"Can't you see he's hurt bad? He needs a doctor. Please..."

The officers helped him up. He had no strength left to fight them anymore. The rain had soaked his clothing through, and his knees were scraped. But he didn't feel the pain.

Charlie reassured him. "We're doing everything we possibly can for him."

He lifted his head to the stars. "Christopher!" His voice cried out like the squealing of a siren. The depth of his pain oozed out into the darkness of the night.

Meanwhile, a distinguished man mysteriously emerged from the crowd and said something to the police officer who'd approached him. Before the officer ran off, he replied, "Yes, Sheriff."

The sheriff walked over to Peter, securely placed his hand on his shoulder, and silently waited for him to compose himself.

"Is he...?" Peter couldn't finish the sentence. It was too painful.

"It's bad."

Looking at the sheriff, he pleaded, "Oh God, no."

He weakly slumped into the sheriff's arms, who led him over to the curb and sat him down. In a compassionate voice, he explained, "I'm sorry. They're doing everything they can for him, but the chances are very slim. The engine is on fire, and the hood is so damaged that we can't get it open to put it out. The firefighters have guaranteed that there won't be an explosion the way things are now, but if it starts leaking gas...."

He didn't want to hear anymore. His husband was in that car, and he needed to be with him now. The sheriff paused, waiting for him to speak. But he couldn't. There were no words to say.

He struggled to find the strength to stand up. The sheriff led him over to the mangled mess of metal.

"You only have a few minutes, so you need to stay calm."

He laid down on his stomach in a pool of rainwater, and got as near to the driver's door as he could.

"Christopher?" He didn't even recognize his own voice. "Christopher, sweetheart?"

Softly and calmly, he reached his hand inside the broken window. But there was more smoke coming from the engine than he'd expected. He misjudged the location of the glass, and it cut his arm. The cut was deep and blood oozed down his arm, but he felt no pain. He was numb.

"Christopher?" He waited a moment, trying to get closer. "Can you hear me, sweetheart?" His voice was soothing and loving.

Pushing his arm further inside, he searched until he could feel the warmth of Christopher's body.

"I'm here now, right beside you. Can you hear me?"

No sound came from inside the car. He pushed his arm in further, and felt a liquid all over his husband's skin. Recoiling, he realized there was blood everywhere. Christopher was saturated in it. He took a deep breath, calmed himself, and tried to talk to him again.

"Christopher, they're going to get you out of there. Everyone is doing everything they can."

His voice choked. He couldn't cry now. He couldn't show weakness, because Christopher needed him to be strong—now more than ever before.

"Christopher, it's all right, sweetheart. Everything is okay."

Then finally, a shallow voice asked, "The baby?"

Controlled and confident, he replied, "She's fine."

"The sitter called and said Catherine wouldn't stop crying— that she was sick. I tried to call you, but I didn't get an answer. So I was turning around to go home and calling your mom to let her know I couldn't make it, and...."

Peter cursed to himself. He should have listened to Christopher and stayed home.

But he continued to talk to him in a calm, affectionate voice. "Catherine is fine. She's sleeping. We're going to get you out of there soon, and the doctors will fix you up. And everything will be just fine."

The smoke from the engine was starting to get to him. His voice didn't sound very convincing anymore. He pulled his arm from the car.

"Christopher, sweetheart, I'll be right back. I need to see where the doctor is. But I won't leave you."

No sound came from inside the car. Standing up, he looked around and shouted, "Someone give me a flashlight!" He looked around as a man raced off into the darkness. "Why is it so smoky? Are you sure the car isn't going to explode?" he asked frantically. "Where are the Jaws of Life?"

He was panicking again. He couldn't understand why everyone was just standing around. Were they just waiting for Christopher to die? He gasped in shock at his own thoughts. What would he do without Christopher? He couldn't die!

He shouted even louder this time. "I want a flashlight, and I want the Jaws of Life here NOW!"

He wanted the night to be erased from time—to never have happened. He ran over to one of the paramedics.

"Why aren't you doing something for him? You need to get him out of there!"

The man touched his arm in a sympathetic manner. He roughly pulled away. He didn't want his sympathy; he wanted his husband. He wanted him out of the car and home safe with him where he belonged. He wanted everything to be the way it was. He wanted Christopher to live.

Suddenly, pain shot through him like a knife slicing him

in two. The paramedic tried to examine the cuts on his arm. He pulled away and snapped, "It's not me you need to attend to. It's my husband. Go help him!"

Charlie, the older officer, walked over, looked at the paramedic, and nodded. The paramedic turned and left, and Charlie spoke slowly and clearly.

"I'm afraid I have very bad news. The Jaws of Life are here now, but it's worse than we thought. Christopher is jammed under the steering wheel, and his body is wrapped around the dash. And metal pieces are lodged...."

Charlie gestured at the mangled mess of metal sitting between the two other vehicles, but Peter just winced at his words. "No, you're wrong. He's going to be all right. He's going to make it!"

Once again, Charlie tried to explain the situation, but Peter wouldn't listen. He didn't want to hear the words.

The paramedic returned. "We can't get him out. If we move him.... The major organs have been ruptured, and there's been a massive loss of blood...."

They kept talking, but it was as if their words were dissolving into the night. Peter was becoming numb and limp. He felt like he was dropping off the edge of a cliff into an abyss. A wave of fatigue overwhelmed him.

He didn't want to believe what he'd been told. Charlie had put his hand on his arm and was guiding him back to Christopher's car. "He doesn't have much longer. The Jaws of Life got through the hood, but the fire has spread so much that they can't completely put it out without fatally injuring him."

And there it was: the proclamation of finality. One way or another, he wasn't going to make it.

Peter felt like he had been kicked so hard that he had no fight left in him. He started wondering what it'd be like to die. The more he thought about it, the more he realized that it didn't matter if he died in the explosion now. Nothing mattered anymore. If Christopher died, so would he. He was his whole life.

Calmly and quietly, he said, "I want to be with him."

"Of course. We'll leave you as long as we can."

"Thank you," he heard himself say in a voice that didn't belong to him.

"You have to wear this," a paramedic said, and held up an oxygen mask.

"But then I won't be able to talk to him."

"If you don't, you'll pass out."

Grudgingly he put on the mask and approached the car. It was sweltering now, and smoke was everywhere. A paramedic adjusted Christopher's oxygen mask, then moved away to give them privacy.

He pushed his arm back inside the smoky car. In a tender voice, he spoke. "Christopher? Sweetheart? Can you hear me?"

He didn't respond, so he ran his hand along his arm to sooth him. He wanted Christopher to know he was there beside him.

A soft murmur escaped Christopher's lips. He brushed his hand against the mask, indicating that he didn't want to wear it. Now Peter felt even more helpless.

Just then, the storm picked up. A gust of wind arose and blew the smoke away from the area immediately surrounding the car, separating them from the officers and paramedics. Since no one could see them and they weren't inhaling smoke anymore, he took off their masks. If they were going to die, he wanted to be able to see Christopher.

But he still couldn't see his face. Nevertheless, he hid his frustration.

"I love you, sweetheart. I'm here now. Everything is going to be okay."

"I'm hurt," Christopher managed to say.

201

"I know, sweetheart. The doctors will be here soon, and they'll make you better."

"I'm hurt bad."

"I know," his voice faded. "I know...."

"Help me," Christopher quietly pleaded.

"I'm trying to, sweetheart. It won't be long now."

He didn't know what else to say. How could he comfort him when he knew Christopher wasn't going to make it? Helplessness set in. He searched his mind for something to say that would make him feel better.

"Christopher? Sweetheart?"

No response.

"Christopher?"

A paramedic approached Peter. The wind had made the smoke clear even more, so they weren't concerned that he'd removed the oxygen masks.

Peter's voice was faint, almost pleading. "He's not responding."

"He's drifting in and out of consciousness. The injuries are bad, and the pain is severe," the paramedic sympathetically replied. "We've done all we can for him. We've given him something to help with the pain. Can you keep talking to him? Make him as comfortable as possible?"

Charlie walked over. "You won't be able to stay here much longer."

"Okay." He was surprised at the lack of emotion in his own reply. The panic was gone, replaced by hopelessness. Loss had already set in.

Christopher was his very breath—his heart and soul. How could God be so cruel? Lumps formed in his throat as he choked back the tears.

"Sir?" Charlie was talking again. "Sir, you only have about

ten minutes. Then we'll have to move back. He's more lucid now. We've told him what's happening, and he—"

"Oh God, why does he have to know? Why couldn't it have been me? I'm not leaving him. Give me a flashlight!" he demanded.

Someone in the crowd ran forward and handed him a flashlight.

Of course, Charlie objected. "I understand how you're—"

"You understand? How could you understand? That's not your partner in there!"

Charlie looked shocked, but Peter didn't care. He wanted everyone to hurt the way he was hurting. Remaining calm, Charlie continued. "It's dangerous, and there's a protocol."

"I'm not leaving," he said in a stronger, more defiant voice, and shot a dirty look at Charlie.

"Okay, okay, relax. We'll do whatever we can to give you more time with your partner."

He got back down on the ground and shined the flashlight into the car. Finally he could see Christopher. His body was wrecked, ghastly, and twisted in an unimaginably horrific way. Blood was oozing down the side of his face. Christopher's eyes fluttered opened, and he slowly looked over at his husband.

Christopher tried to smile at him. "Hi, Peter."

He smiled back at Christopher, but his heartache was unbearable. Even now, he couldn't help but think about how handsome he was. "Hi," he softly replied.

"Fine mess we're in, huh?" Christopher tried to giggle. But he coughed, and blood trickled out of the side of his mouth.

"It's okay, Christopher. We'll fix this. You'll see."

"Not sure…." His voice had a rough, chalky sound to it.

"Not sure about what, sweetheart?"

A few moments passed before Christopher answered. "Not

sure you can fix this one."

Again he tried to laugh, but the pain was too great.

"Don't talk, Kit. It hurts too much. I'm here with you. That's all that matters now."

"I'm not going to make it, am I?"

He swallowed hard before answering. He needed him to believe that everything was going to be all right. The night seemed to soften.

"Now who's silly?" He tried to sound lighthearted. "Of course you're going to make it. Catherine is at home waiting for you, and I'm right here. You're going to be just fine. You'll just be in there a few more minutes...."

He pressed Christopher's arm harder to reassure him. He knew he was a lousy liar.

"It's okay, Peter. I know I'm not going to make it. Promise me you'll look after Catherine. Make sure she grows up happy." Christopher choked as the blood clogged in his throat. "Promise me," he desperately pleaded. It was obviously excruciatingly painful to speak. "Promise!"

"I promise, sweetheart." Peter's words were suffocated by an emptiness he'd never felt before. He remembered their dreams about growing old together. They'd sit on the porch, surrounded by their children and grandchildren, and tell stories about their life together. They'd hold hands and look at each other like it was their wedding day; they'd never lose the magic.

It wasn't supposed to end this way. It was all wrong.

Christopher sensed his agony. "It's okay, Peter. It all happened so fast. I just wish I could've had more time with you and Catherine."

"Don't talk like that."

"Shhh, sweetheart. You have to be brave now, for Catherine."

He tried to think of something to take Christopher's mind off the pain. "Do you remember our honeymoon? And all the times we sat in the backyard under the stars and reminisced about our wedding day?"

Christopher loved to hear him talk about how much he was in love with him.

"You were so handsome. I couldn't believe that you'd marry me."

"But I did," Christopher lovingly murmured.

Suddenly, his emotions burst forward. "Christopher, I love you so much!"

"Tell me about our honeymoon again," Christopher weakly whispered. "I want to hear it from your lips one last time."

Christopher started to fade away, so he quickly took a deep breath and began: "The wedding was wonderful, but the best part was when we were finally alone. Then I realized that you were truly mine. Do you remember, Christopher?"

Christopher smiled and closed his eyes. "Yes."

"We were driving off down the road, remember?"

Christopher didn't reply.

"I pulled off to the side of the road. You wondered what I was doing.... Christopher?" Peter sat bolt upright. "Christopher?" Disoriented, he listened for his voice.

The storm had died down, making the smoke and heat exponentially more intense. Sweat was pouring down Peter's face.

"Oh God!" Hiding his head in his hands, he started crying uncontrollably. The pain in his heart was unbearable. The extreme conditions overcame him, and he slipped into unconsciousness.

CHAPTER 33
THE WEDDING NIGHT

The car swerved to the side of the road, leaving a skidding gravel sound as it abruptly stopped.

"What's wrong?" Christopher asked, surprised.

Peter turned off the ignition and got out of the car. "I'll be back in a minute." He got out and walked around the back of the car and down the road behind them.

Christopher didn't know what was happening and started to worry.

Suddenly his door opened, and there was his husband. Peter knelt on one knee and looked deeply into Christopher's eyes. Christopher smiled back. Peter took his hand in his and kissed it. Then he presented Christopher with a small bouquet of wildflowers, which he'd just picked from the side of the road. Christopher loved wildflowers, and was deeply touched by this simple gesture of love.

"Thank you." Tears of happiness welled up in Christopher's eyes.

"I'll surprise you every day of our lives. I promise." Christopher looked at him with tenderness. "Together, we can accomplish anything."

Christopher started crying. Peter kissed his hand, stood up, and gently pulled him out of the car. They kissed with more passion than either one of them knew existed.

"I love you so much," Peter whispered.

"I love you more." Christopher paused. "Don't ever leave me, or my heart will die."

"I won't. I promise," he whispered as he held Christopher even tighter. "This is true love, made in heaven."

CHAPTER 34
THE EXPLOSION

"Made in heaven," he mumbled as he awoke. He realized he was on the ground, covered in gasoline. He didn't want to open his eyes and face reality. Finally, he reached over, found Christopher's hand, and kissed it.

"Don't ever leave me, or my heart will die," he whispered.

"I won't ever leave you, Peter," Christopher choked. "I'll live in your heart forever."

Then he closed his eyes.

"Sir?" It was Charlie. "Sir?"

Peter turned his head to look up at him.

"I'm sorry, but you have to move away from the car now. You passed out from the smoke, and the engine is leaking gas. It's a miracle you're not on fire already."

"How can I leave him?"

"I know, sir, but your life is at stake."

"Please."

"I'm sorry, but you'll have to come with me now," Charlie repeated more firmly.

Christopher seemed to be sleeping. The pained look on his

208

face had faded.

Peter tried to reach into the car again, but Charlie pulled him away. He ripped himself out of his grip, but several officers grabbed him and restrained him. He lashed out at them with his fists.

"Let me go," he shouted in a rage. "Let me die with him." He struggled relentlessly. "Damn you. Damn you all."

"I'm so sorry," Charlie said soothingly.

"I love you so much, Christopher. Please forgive me." Tears were blurring his vision now. They streamed uncontrollably down his face. "I love you!"

His pain oozed into the night, touching all those present.

He kept struggling, but the officers pulled him away from the car. The instant they'd cleared the area, the car exploded.

Nevertheless, he broke away from them again and tried to return to Christopher. But the impact caused by the explosion stopped him in his tracks, making his hair fly back. He felt like a bird flying into the wind.

Finally, he stopped. He was frozen to the spot, shocked at the sight of fire booming high above the car, then falling to the ground.

Long and hard, he cried out into the darkness. "Christopher!"

The high-pitched inhuman sound of his pain and anguish would never be forgotten by everyone who could hear it. He slumped to the ground, limp and lifeless. The sound echoed through the emptiness of the night as the fire lit up the coal-black sky.

CHAPTER 35
THE ANSWER

Pain shot through his body. He shivered from the dampness of the morning. In the distance, he could hear the helicopter taking off. He was relieved that his men had made it to safety.

He could hear the enemy closing in. Soon it would be time. Lying still against the log, he waited.

Then a faint figure appeared in the fog, but it wasn't an enemy soldier. Straining his eyes through his pain, he tried to clear his blurry vision. A small white form elegantly drifted toward him in the mist.

"Christopher?"

He reached out to touch him. Christopher looked so handsome, standing there in his white satin pajamas, the morning light reflecting off his dark wavy hair. He wanted to gently touch his tan skin, run his fingers down his neck, and smell his cologne.

"I couldn't save you," he murmured.

"We'll be together again before you know it, Peter," Christopher sweetly whispered as he caressed his cheek.

He grabbed Christopher's hand, holding it tightly against his face. "I'm not going to make it home."

"Home is wherever I am," Christopher said reassuringly.

He smiled, reached into his pocket, and pulled out the harmonica that his father had given him.

"Remember when we danced to this at our wedding?"

The song was "I'll Be Loving You Always." He played it from his heart, and when he was finished, he looked up.

Christopher's form had faded, and the old woman had taken his place. He frowned.

"Where did Christopher go? Why are you here, old woman?"

His words were harsher than he'd intended. And the old woman's familiar words came back at him even harsher. "What can a bird do to stop the wind?"

Then her form faded into the darkness of the dawn. He realized he was delirious. All that was left was the sound of the enemy crushing through the debris in the woods.

Blood ran down his chin. When he heard himself choking on it, his mind returned to the night of the accident.

He'd replayed what happened over and over in his mind. He'd felt so helpless that he wanted to die with his husband.

But in the days following the accident, he started to realize that he'd been surrounded by people who'd devoted their lives to trying to save people — even when it was futile, and it put their lives at stake. Eventually, he decided that he would do the same thing, and that's when he enlisted.

And in that moment, he had the answer: That's what a bird could do to the stop the wind. His life hadn't been in vain. Even though he couldn't save Christopher or keep his promise about Catherine, he'd devoted the rest of his life to trying to save those who needed to be protected.

He tried to push the harmonica back into his pocket. Picking up his rifle, he positioned it on the log in front of him.

The old woman's smiling face appeared. He smiled back at

211

her and nodded. Then she disappeared.

The enemy soldiers were moving in closer. He could hear their voices now. Every nerve in his body was twitching. Then he heard a rustling behind him, so he threw some pebbles into the bushes to confuse the enemy. They shot a few rounds in his direction, not knowing how many soldiers were waiting for them.

Finally, he saw an enemy soldier in the dim of the morning light. This time, it was clear that the form he saw was no delusion.

A strength came over him as he perched himself against the old fallen log. He lifted his rifle and began to fire. He shot as many of the enemy soldiers as he could, but soon, too many of their bullets pelted into his body.

He fell against the log with a smile on his face. His heart and soul were finally at peace. He was going home.

CHAPTER 36
THE FORGOTTEN

In the morning light, the chopper landed. The troop had safely returned to camp. The medics rushed the wounded to the tented area that awaited them.

Then Browning headed to his C.O. to make his report. When he was finished, he stood up and saluted, requesting that he be allowed to take some soldiers and a chopper back to get Sarge's body. His C.O. informed him that he should be able to grant his request soon, since the information that Sarge's pictures supplied would in all likelihood result in the freedom of the prisoners.

Indeed, two days later, the enemy camp was destroyed, and the prisoners were freed. So Browning was given permission to return and check on Sarge.

Browning found Sarge exactly where he'd left him. His wrecked body, which had been riddled with bullets, was laden with flies. His sticky blood had congealed, leaving the stench of decay.

He was propped up on a log, his rifle in one hand and Christopher's picture in the other. Some of the soldiers were surprised to find out that he was gay, but none of them said

213

anything because they didn't want to disrespect his memory. His harmonica and a letter to Catherine rested on the ground beside him. Strange as it may sound, Browning swore he could see a smile on his mutilated face.

Browning picked up Sarge's belongings and gave the grim order. The men silently carried his body down the hill to the waiting chopper. As they boarded the chopper and headed back to camp, no one spoke.

The men were shipped to Germany, where they awaited their release orders. They should've been happy, but they were filled with sadness, which they carried with them for a long time. Each one of them had grown to love their sergeant. He was a good, brave man, and he'd sacrificed his life for them. He had looked after them as he'd promised he would.

CHAPTER 37
THE ACHING

Days turned into weeks, and weeks into months. And there had still been no word from her Stone Soldier.

Before she knew it, it was New Year's Eve. That night, a blanket of darkness crept upon the horizon. The flickering of candlelight in the window melodically swayed like a soprano singing a sonata.

Leaning on the railing of the patio, she stared out into the vast darkness. She was wrapped in the silence of the night. Long ago she'd printed out her soldier's email, which she now held in her hand. "How many times have I read this?" she pondered.

The golden light of the moon danced on the crispness of the air. The sky was blanketed with stars. The gently falling snowflakes danced like magic gleams. It was an amazingly beautiful sight, yet she felt numb.

She was ambiguously aware of the consequences of standing out in the cold too long, yet she was frozen in time. Her heart silently cried for her Stone Soldier. Such pain. Her mind was oblivious to everything happening around her; thoughts of him occupied all of her thoughts.

Everything they'd talked about during those months made sense now. She had a new clarity about his state of mind. Through the pages she held in her hand, his life looked black and white.

As she kept staring out into the coldness of the night, she had no thoughts of comfort or wisdom, just a pain that had sunk deep inside her. In that moment, she truly understood what sympathy pain was: she was aching because of his suffering. She longed to hear from him one more time. Where could he be?

Suddenly, fireworks filled the sky like diamonds. It was midnight. They flickered and flashed with great beauty, but she felt nothing about the entering of the New Year. Tiredness overtook her, so she turned and went inside.

The email her soldier had sent her was so much more than she was expecting. It was more than anyone could've imagined. Now she knew his secret, which gave her quite a feeling of power.

Every day for months she'd reread his email. Every day she hoped to hear that he was safe at home with Catherine. She wanted him to be happy — to have the life of his dreams. Had he become an English teacher, as he so desperately wanted?

It some ways, it was easier to believe that his dreams had come true. In her mind she could believe that he was celebrating his new life at that moment. He was holding Catherine tightly in his arms as they watched fireworks from his patio. He was loving her with all his heart, as he'd promised Christopher he would that tragic night.

So that New Year's Eve, she made a decision: That's what had happened to him. He'd gone on with his life, and forgotten about this stranger on the computer. She settled for that explanation. She had to. She didn't want to think about the other possibility. Believing he was happy was so much more comforting.

CHAPTER 38
THE BOOK SIGNING

Edward bent over and whispered quietly, "Olivia, it's time to wrap it up. You're tired, and you've done enough for today."

"I know. Just a couple more, okay?"

Olivia hated to disappoint her fans. After all, if readers weren't buying her book, she wouldn't be signing it in Pacific Centre at her favorite bookstore.

Edward wasn't happy about her decision, but he nodded in agreement. He didn't like how Olivia looked lately; she was pale and wan. She wasn't sleeping, and he knew why: the dreams with the old woman and the soldier had returned. They'd haunted her for a long time now.

Olivia took the book from the next man in line and mechanically asked, "What inscription would you like me to write?"

She looked up and smiled.

"Sign it to Jacob, please," replied the tall red-headed man smiling down at her. "I love your book about the Stone Soldier. I can't wait to read your next one."

"Thank you, Jacob. I'm glad you enjoyed it. I wrote it for a person who's very special to me."

Olivia took the pen and neatly wrote,

To Jacob,
Fond wishes,
Olivia

How many autographs had she signed? Edward was right; she was feeling very tired. The book tour had lasted long enough. It was time to pack it up and head back to her quiet home on Denman Island. She was supposed to be on holiday, not promoting her book. At least that was the idea when she'd decided to come here.

But when Coles had tasked her to do a reading, she just couldn't refuse. After all, British Columbia was her home territory, and she felt compelled to be faithful to it.

She'd been traveling nonstop across Canada for weeks now. After some rest on Denman Island, she'd be ready to start writing her next novel. She had no idea what she was going to write about, but Edward had talked her into signing another contract with the publishing company. And her deadline was less than six months away. Olivia sighed, feeling like a fool.

The red-headed man seemed pleased as Olivia mechanically handed his book back to him. She once again reached for her pen, and without looking up, she motioned for the next person in line. "What inscription would you like me to write?"

The young woman who was next in line answered slowly and unconfidently. "Could you please write…? I'm not sure."

Suddenly, Olivia had a sick, twisted feeling in her stomach. She knew something was going to happen, but she wasn't sure what. The young woman had long, wavy black hair, which flowed gently around her tiny heart-shaped face. She was about eighteen years old, tall, and stunningly beautiful.

Olivia stared at her. She knew her somehow, but she couldn't place her. The young woman gave her a sweet smile.

"Have we met before?" Olivia probingly asked.

"Well, sort of. But not exactly."

Olivia looked puzzled. Perhaps she was just one of her fans. After all, she'd met so many people during the book tour that she couldn't keep track of anyone anymore.

"I loved your book."

"Thank you."

"It was so…real."

It seemed like the young woman was trying to clue Olivia in, but she was still stumped.

"Who would you like me to make it out to?" Perhaps hearing her name would jog her memory.

"Could you…? I mean, if you don't mind…." The young girl hesitated, then swallowed hard, as if she was about to reveal a huge secret. "Could you sign, 'In memory of the Stone Soldier'?"

Olivia just stared at the young woman. She was in shock. She kept trying to find the words, but they were stuck in her throat.

The young woman slid her hardcover copy slowly towards Olivia, who was still frozen in her seat.

"Did you know him?" Olivia finally asked, quietly and slowly.

"He was my father."

Olivia was visibly jarred by this statement. "Catherine?"

A delighted smile crossed the beautiful young woman's face. "Yes."

So many times Olivia had imagined that this meeting might occur. She desperately wanted it to, but she never really believed that it would. And now here she was. It was really happening.

Olivia's face grew even paler. The emotion of the moment exacerbated her exhaustion.

Again, Edward was whispering in her ear. "Are you okay?"

"Yes, I'm fine." Olivia brushed him off, then took the book from Catherine. Her heart was racing. "So is there a particular name you'd like me to sign it to? I mean, I never knew your father's real name. We didn't...."

"I know. I read your emails."

Olivia put the pen down.

"How?"

"I.... He...." Catherine was clearly upset.

"You don't have to tell me right now."

"Okay."

"You don't know how many times I wish we'd exchanged names." Olivia's eyes filled with tears, but she tried not to cry.

"He loved you like a second mother. At least that's what he wrote in his journal."

"He did?" Olivia was overwhelmed.

"The dreams you gave him helped him get through a lot of things."

"Catherine?"

"Yes?"

"What was his name?" she asked softly and compassionately. "I never knew...." She held her breath in anticipation.

"Peter."

Olivia smiled. "Of course. Peter."

She started writing, making sure every word — every letter — expressed the way she was feeling at that moment.

To Peter, My Stone Soldier,

For your bravery and compassion, and for the love and friendship you so freely gave me. Without you, I could never have written this book.

Love,
Olivia

Then she shut the book, but left one hand on it, as if to guard it.

She motioned for Edward to come closer and whispered, "Please apologize to everyone for me. Make up an excuse, anything. I need to take a break."

Edward was relieved. He knew she needed a vacation. In fact, it was long overdue. And he was excited about seeing Catherine in the flesh. In fact, he'd had a tough time not saying something earlier. "You got it!"

"Pack everything up. Then we'll head to Denman Island."

"No problem."

Olivia motioned for Catherine to follow her. Catherine picked up her book and followed her to the back of the bookstore, where they disappeared into a small office.

Olivia still couldn't believe it. She looked exactly like Peter's description of Christopher.

Catherine was the first to speak. "I needed to meet you."

Olivia kept looking at her like she'd seen a ghost.

Catherine was getting nervous now. "I hope you don't mind."

Still no answer from Olivia.

"Perhaps this was a mistake." Catherine turned to leave.

"No. No, I'm sorry. I just...."

Catherine turned back toward Olivia, who stepped forward, grabbed her, and hugged her tightly.

Finally, Olivia let her tears escape. "I'm sorry. It's just.... Seeing you standing there...."

"I know." Catherine was feeling it too. It was like they knew each other, yet they'd never met. And now all the pain and sorrow seemed to flow through their veins, bringing back memories that'd been locked away in their hearts.

They hugged each other for a long time.

Olivia was the first to speak. "Catherine, I know this is hard.

But I need to ask."

"It's okay. I figured you would," Catherine gently replied. "My father was killed in action—on his last mission. He got a medal of bravery."

Olivia grabbed hold of the back of a chair and slowly lowered herself into it. In her heart, she'd always known that her soldier had gotten killed. But nevertheless, all those years, she'd hoped that he'd somehow made it. After all, he'd been so adamant about making it up to Catherine.

"I knew.... The mission...." The words were like lumps in Olivia's throat.

Catherine had tears in her eyes. "It's okay, Olivia. I'm very proud of my father. I never got to meet him, but I have this picture."

Catherine pulled a photo out of her pocket and handed it to Olivia. She hesitated at first. Was she ready to see his face? Ultimately, the awkwardness of the moment trumped her indecisiveness, and she took the photo.

"He's even more handsome than I thought."

"I love that picture."

"I can see why. So how did you read our conversations?"

"They were with his other belongings when they brought him home to New York. When I was thirteen, I was having a lot of emotional problems. So my grandparents decided that it was time for me to have his belongings. They thought I was too young to understand everything when he died, so they kept it hidden until then."

Catherine paused to collect herself, then continued.

"The harmonica that my grandfather had given him was inside the box, as well as some letters from my grandmother. And there was a sealed letter that my father had written to me, apologizing for not being there for me after my mother died. It had a stamp on it. I guess my dad never had the chance to mail it. One of his soldiers delivered it to our home. I think his last name was Browning."

Catherine took a moment to wipe tears from her eyes.

"There were also several discs. Your emails and instant messages were on those discs. He kept everything you wrote to him. And then there were his journal writings. They explained a lot. I discovered just how important you were to him. You gave him hopes and dreams that enabled him to overcome his disappointments: in humanity and in himself. I found out how much he loved my other father, and how deep his grief was after his death."

When Catherine paused again, Olivia addressed what she'd been wondering since she laid eyes on her.

"I want to ask you something, but I don't want to pry."

"Ask away."

"How do you look like Christopher?"

To Olivia's surprise, Catherine wasn't even jarred by the question. She'd obviously rattled off this explanation a million times. It actually seemed like a reprieve from the emotional conversation.

"My dads wanted to have a biological child, rather than adopt. So they asked their friend to be a surrogate mother, and they decided to use Christopher for the insemination. But she died during childbirth."

"So much death," Olivia mournfully recalled.

"I know. So when I read your journal, I finally understood why he'd left me with my grandparents. For the first time, I wasn't angry at him. Suddenly, everything just made so much sense. In my heart, I knew I definitely wanted to meet the stranger who'd talked to my father on the computer night after night—the woman that'd kept his hope alive. I knew I needed to meet you."

223

Catherine's eyes were red from crying, and her cheeks were flushed from all the emotion she was feeling. Olivia took Catherine's hands in hers and gently held them.

"Catherine, your father was a wonderful man. He opened his heart to me. He allowed me to see all the love and pain and confusion he was feeling. I was very lucky to have shared those moments with him. He wanted to come home to you so deeply. He loved you very much."

Catherine continued Olivia's train of thought. "And I know you loved him like a mother loves her own child. Your love helped him get through those dark days, and I can never thank you enough for that. I just wish that...."

Tears choked in her throat. Olivia hugged her, and together they cried for Peter.

After a while, Olivia asked, "So how did you find me?"

Catherine smiled. "Everything was there in your conversations with my father."

Olivia looked puzzled.

"The dreams you gave my father told me exactly where to look for you: the pond, the ocean. You even told him the name of the island where you grew up. Remember, I knew everything about you that my father did. I just didn't have your real name, and your screenname had been deleted by then."

"I couldn't keep it anymore. It just hurt too much. The memories...."

"That's what I thought had happened. When I was applying to medical schools, I remembered how kind you'd been to my father, and thought that might be indicative of the people in this area. And their research about brain cancer at the University of British Columbia is some of the most advanced in the world, and that's what I want to specialize in."

"Just like Christopher," added Olivia.

"He used to call himself the Florence Nightingale of brain treatment," Catherine jokingly agreed.

After they finished laughing, Catherine continued.

"Then a few weeks ago, I needed a break from medical school, so I came here— downtown. And when I passed Coles, there it was, advertised in the store window: *The Stone Soldier*. I remembered the nickname from your conversations, so I instantly knew that it was about my father. And not only that, there was an announcement about you doing a reading in a few weeks. So here I am."

"I don't know what to say, Catherine. Since I never heard from your father, I didn't know what'd happened. And of course I didn't want to think the worst. So I dreamt that he was happy at home with his beautiful daughter. And to work through my feelings, I wrote my book. I never dreamed it would ever get published. But one day, I met Edward through a friend of mine, and we started talking. He was quite taken by the story, and sent it to a publisher friend of his. And the rest is history."

Olivia paused.

"I'm sorry I wrote a happy ending."

"No, I loved it!" Catherine squeezed Olivia's hand. "It was beautiful. My father would've loved it too. It was exactly how he wanted his life to turn out."

"You really think so?"

"Yes, it was his dream to be a teacher, and you made it come true for him."

Olivia thought about Peter. She finally knew her Stone Soldier's name: Peter.

"Catherine?"

"Yes?"

"Would you like to come and stay with me on Denman Island for a few days? I want to show you my home. I can't show it to...

Peter. But I'd love to show you. You could take the BC Ferries out of Horse Shoe Bay to Nanaimo, and I could pick you up there and take you back to my house. Denman Island is just an hour north of there. It's a lot cheaper than renting a car or taking a bus."

Catherine smiled through her tears. "Yes, I'd like that very much."

Olivia hugged Catherine tightly. Her Stone Soldier had finally been laid to rest. She knew the end of his story, and that was all that mattered.

About the Author

Tossia Mitchell is a novelist, poet, and short-story writer. She has also written articles that have been published in various newspapers. She holds degrees from Douglas College and the University of Northern British Columbia.

Tossia was raised on gorgeous Denman Island in British Columbia. Her father was a Sargent Major in the British Army during WWII; he was on the beach on D-Day. Tossia's husband Gary was the head chocolatier for Purdy's in Vancouver until he recently passed away.

As a behavior interventionist, Tossia works with children with autism and delayed speech. She owns her own business and privately sees 25 students every week.

CPSIA information can be obtained
at www.ICGtesting.com
Printed in the USA
LVOW12s0506070318

568934LV00001B/2/P